To Dave~
Thanks f
Suppor ♥ Nov

# Cross My Heart

Natalie Vivien

ROSE + STAR Press

## Books by Natalie Vivien

*The Vampire Next Door* (with Bridget Essex)
*Heart-Shaped Box*
*French Lessons*
*Drawn to You*
*Love Stories*
*The Ghost of a Chance*
*Falling for Hope*
*The Thousand Mile Love Story*
*For the Love of Indiana*

## About the Author

Natalie Vivien writes love stories, because she lives a love story that inspires her every day. Together with her wife, author Bridget Essex, for over a decade and married for over eight years, they are madly and passionately in love, and build a good, cozy life together with several fur babies who get away with murder because they're so adorable.

Natalie and Bridget founded Rose and Star Press in 2014, a publisher of lesbian romance and fiction of distinction. Lesbian romance is Natalie's life's work, and she hopes very much that you enjoyed *Cross My Heart*.

Learn more about Natalie at **http://natalievivien.wordpress.com** or send her an email at **miss.natalie.vivien@gmail.com**.

Learn more about Rose and Star Press, publishers of lesbian romance and fiction of distinction, at **http:///www.LesbianRomance.org**

Cross My Heart
Copyright © 2015 Natalie Vivien
All Rights Reserved
Published by Rose and Star Press
First edition, September 2015

This is a work of fiction. Names, characters, places and incidents
either are products of the author's imagination or are used
fictitiously. Any resemblance to actual events or locales or persons,
living or dead, is entirely coincidental.

This book, or parts thereof, may not be reproduced without
written permission.

ISBN-13: 978-1977993335
ISBN-10: 1977993338

# Cross My Heart

*Dedication:*
B. Yours forever.  Cross my heart.  N.

# Chapter One

"Welcome to Bean Power! Would you like to try our new Mega Mondo Mochaccino, ma'am?"

As I regard the barista with bleary, jet-lagged eyes and try to make sense of his alliteration, my sunglasses slip down a notch, causing the coffee shop to appear half sepia-toned and half bright, clashing Technicolor. The walls are tiled with green and orange glass squares, and there's a pink paper bunting strung up behind the coffee bar area proclaiming BEAN POWER in die-cut turquoise letters. The staff is outfitted in tie-dye t-shirts and acid-washed jeans, and at the center of every table, lava lamps ooze glowy purple globs.

"Mega what?" I ask, squinting and shoving my shades back into place. I wobble on my legs a little, still queasy from the flight.

"Mondo Mochaccino! Quite the tongue-twister, I know." The barista's grin is sweeter, I'd wager, than that bottle of Sugar-Shock Syrup sitting on the shelf above his shoulder. "It's infused with our brand-new Choco-Wow blend, six shots of espresso, topped off with shaved dark chocolate and a swirl of caramel. Best of all, it comes in a refillable—and recyclable—48-ounce cup. All you can drink!" He holds up a hand and begins ticking items off. "We've recently expanded our milk offerings, so I can make you the Mega Mondo Mochaccino with cow's milk, non-fat cow's milk, goat's milk, soy milk, almond milk, rice milk, coconut milk, hemp milk—"

"No, no, thanks. No milk. No Mondo Choco…anything. Please." I grimace and try to ignore the roiling feeling in my stomach. The scents of onion-and-cheese paninis on the grill, sickly sweet beverages, and patchouli incense waft heavily around me.

My stomach shudders, and I close my eyes, willing the nausea away.

And I promise myself, not for the first time, that I am *never* traveling by plane again.

There's a reason I've dedicated my life to archaeology. Digging in the earth, I feel peaceful, grounded. *Safe.* The sky and I, on the other hand, don't get along so well. My first plane ride, when I was three years old, resulted in a two-bucket mop-up of the center aisle of first class. And things got significantly worse for the unlucky attendants assigned to my flights as the years wore on.

When I was fourteen, I threw up on the bald head of the man seated in front of me—who just happened to be the field manager of my father's dig site in Cairo. The guy had no patience for children and was, oddly enough, a little superstitious. He held a grudge against Dad for bringing me to Egypt for years, blaming my presence on the disappointing site excavation. Apparently my poetry-reading, black-clad teenage self scared the undiscovered relics away.

But I definitely broke my personal nausea record on this last flight: *five* bulging "courtesy bags" handed over to the flight attendant before the plane touched ground at Buffalo Niagara International Airport. I wince now, remembering the pained expression on the flight attendant's face when I pressed the call button yet *again* to summon her to dispose of my sick. The woman seated next to me will probably have a permanent crick in her neck from leaning so hard away from my retching self.

It'll be a long, *long* time before I consume solid food again…or anything thicker than coffee. I probably shouldn't even drink the coffee, but I've got a hard day ahead of me, and I'm operating on Egyptian time and about six minutes of sleep.

"Gonna pass on the special, huh?" The barista's smile dims from 1,000 watts to a muted 800, but it's still wide enough that my own cheek muscles begin to ache in sympathy. "All right. No big. There's always next time. Well, what can I get for you today, ma'am?"

I draw my wallet out of my bag—or I try to, but my sleepy hands produce my passport, a magnifying glass, a rolled-up gum wrapper, and a packet of tissues in slow succession. The barista continues to gaze at me with infinite, inhuman patience. When I finally locate my wallet—an old embroidered pouch that Dad bought for me in Peru—I unzip it and dig out a crinkled five-dollar bill. "I need coffee. Just coffee—"

"Of course! Just coffee. A good old cup of Joe. I'll have that right up for you." He taps a button on the cash register in front of him; then he lifts his eyes to meet mine, tilting his head of long bottle-green hair to one side. "So," he smiles, "would you prefer the Sumatra blend, the Tuscan blend, the Parisian Crème, the Desert Siesta—"

"Sorry, I don't mean to be rude. But, honestly, I don't care what you put in my cup, as long as it's as thin as water and as strong as hell. Okay?"

"Oh…" He looks startled for a moment, but

then his shoulders relax, and his mouth slides into a more natural-looking smirk. "Ohhh-kay, the Desert Siesta it is." He chuckles to himself and leans toward me conspiratorially. "Hey, don't tell the boss, but my co-workers and I call this blend Puddle, because it looks and tastes like a mud puddle in a coffee cup. How's that sound? Up your alley?"

"Yeah, perfect." I sigh, but the sigh turns, of its own accord, into a yawn. I shake my head again, widening my eyes to try to force them to stay open.

"Want it black?"

"Please." I accept my change and anxiously await the presentation of my scalding hot, mud-puddly beverage. It's been twelve hours since I've consumed caffeine in any form, and my body—and brain—are staging an internal civil war. *Tomorrow*, I keep telling myself. *Tomorrow I can sleep in.*

Or, hey, maybe I'll sleep *all* day long. The thought of sleep is so enticing that my muscles begin to sag; I lean against the order counter to help me stay on my feet.

*Get it together, Alex.* Today... Today there's mortgage paperwork to sign, a dilapidated house to make superficially inhabitable, a life to start over from, more or less, square one.

Part of me is excited to begin again, to reinvent myself in a new place. But a deeper part of me is already missing the desert and the untethered lifestyle that I chose to leave behind.

There's no need to feel trapped, though—or so I've been telling myself over and over again, ever since I made that fateful call to Rainbow Realty. This is only temporary. Everything in life—my life, anyway—is temporary, just another crazy venture before the *next* crazy venture.

"Are you on your way to the falls?" the barista asks over his shoulder, as he begins to fill my brown paper cup at the coffee station. "Where are you staying?"

God, I must look like a tourist. I'm wearing a neon pink *Niagara Falls* t-shirt, purchased hastily at the airport gift shop after I realized that the airline lost my luggage somewhere between Cairo and New York. I felt too grungy to face the world in my rumpled clothes, and this t-shirt was the only one in my size in the bargain bin at NY Souvenirs For You—and it still cost twenty-five bucks.

"Actually," I say, smiling faintly, "I just bought a house here, over on Cascade Avenue."

"Cascade?" The barista's eyebrows raise—and it's not a good kind of a raise, not a "Wow, that's impressive! Way to go!" raise. It's the sort of two-brow raise that people give you when you come out of the bathroom with your skirt tucked into your pantyhose waistband.

He lowers his gaze for a moment, as if he's trying to think of something positive to say, but the best he can conjure up is, "You sure it's Cascade? Not Carver or—I don't know—Christenson? Cascade... Last I heard, that whole street was condemned."

"Really?" I blink; then I frown, doubtful. "Can a *street* be condemned?"

"When it's Cascade Avenue, it can," he replies dryly. In one practiced motion, he fills my cup to the rim without spilling a drop and reaches for a biodegradable lid. "Man, the stories I've heard about that road—"

"What kind of stories?"

He stares at me uncertainly, a lopsided grin playing over his lips. "Well, you've got the news reports—about drug deals and gangs. But then there's the *weird* stuff. Buddy of mine tried squatting in one of the abandoned houses there, this big Victorian with a purple door—"

"A purple door?" Eyes widening, I clear my throat and lean in a little closer, fingers gripping the edge of the countertop. "Yeah? So, what happened?"

"He didn't make it through the night. Around eleven, Mike showed up at my apartment, white as a freaking *ghost*. Said *he* saw a ghost floating down the staircase."

"He saw a—what?" I take a step back from the counter and reflexively cross my arms over my chest, covering up the blaring *Niagara Falls* logo. "Wait. You mean... He claims the house is haunted?"

"Hey, I don't know. Mike's a pretty straight-up guy, and he was genuinely scared, so..." The barista pauses and stares at me, green hair dangling in front of his eyes. "Hold on. Oh, no *way*. Don't tell me *you* bought the Victorian with the purple door?"

I bite my lip and, reluctantly, nod my head. "Afraid so." I force a smile, shrugging my shoulders slightly, and then I uncross my arms, positioning my hands on my hips. "But I don't believe in ghosts."

"Ah, the Scully type."

"Hmm?"

"You're a skeptic, huh?"

I draw in a slow breath, considering. "I'm a scientist. And I've never experienced convincing evidence of anything paranormal—"

The barista laughs. "Definitely a Scully type. Well, for your sake, I hope you can remain a nonbeliever. Because seriously? I've *never* seen anyone so scared in my life. Poor guy. He's still afraid to sleep with the lights off. Bought him a Snoopy nightlight for his birthday as a gag gift. All right, here's your Puddle."

I yawn again as the barista hands me my coffee in a cardboard sleeve illustrated with an anthropomorphized coffee bean proclaiming, "Try our new Mega Mondo Mochaccino! It's Mega Mondo delicious!" The coffee bean's wearing a tie-dyed t-shirt, like the ones the coffee shop employees wear, with stick-figure arms popping out of his short sleeves. I vaguely recall having seen his likeness on one of the billboards the cab drove me past on the trip here from the airport. With that sort of a publicity campaign, this café must be part of a chain. Starbucks has a mermaid logo; Bean Power has a hippie coffee bean. Makes sense, I guess.

"Enjoy your Desert Siesta."

"I've had my fill of the desert for a while," I say, offering the barista a watery smile. "But thanks for the coffee."

My tired feet shuffle me out of the café and into the warm, bright afternoon air. It's early autumn, and the trees lining the street have just begun to lose their green; their veins and tips are smudged with scarlet and gold. I've been overseas, bound in every direction by desert dunes for so long, that I'd forgotten about autumn, about seasons.

I'd forgotten about a lot of things.

Shaking my head again—to wake myself up as much as to chase away unwelcome thoughts—I start walking along the narrow, unkempt sidewalk. The house is within walking distance of the café. I'd asked the taxi driver to drop me off in this shopping plaza, about half a mile from my final destination, because I wanted to come upon my new residence slowly, not suddenly. I wanted to be able to take it in inch by inch, as if I were unearthing a potsherd or a little statue from the dirt.

Corny as it sounds, I want to discover it, like the proverbial diamond in the rough. As much as I protest that I'm a scientist, that I am, heart and soul, my practical-minded father's daughter, I'd be lying if I denied inheriting some of my mother's romanticism. Over the years, I've published hundreds of articles and contributed dozens of artifacts to worldwide museums, but part of me is still hoping to find *it*—that big, *huge* discovery, an undeniable treasure, tantamount to King Tut's tomb or Mary Anning's prehistoric revelations on the English seacoast.

But when I turn left onto Cascade Avenue—taking in the hollowed-out factories and vacant lots littered with trash—and come upon the two-story Victorian a few minutes later, its angular shape set back several feet from the road and shadowed by pines with untamed, shaggy branches, the word *treasure* doesn't immediately—or even eventually—come to mind. I'm so stunned by the sight that the coffee cup slips out of my grasp; muddy brown coffee pours from the lid, staining the broken sidewalk and splashing on my boots. No great loss there: my boots were already filthy. I should toss them, I know, but they've crossed the globe with me, my only consistent traveling companions, and I've grown a little sentimental about the smelly old things.

"Welcome…home?" I whisper, my voice gravelly with disbelief and more than a little alarm.

I haven't drunk enough caffeine to deal with

this. Part of me wants to just turn away, hail another cab, and high-tail it back to the airport, buy a plane ticket for anywhere—anywhere *else*—and to hell with my airsickness. But my curiosity gets the better of me, and I take a step closer, tilting my head back to peer up at the odd, rusty weathervane on the shingled roof. It almost looks like…a dinosaur?

I'd only seen three photos of the property before purchasing it—all of them faraway, aerial views, taken by helicopter, I guess—and none of those photos prepared me for this brittle, toppling-over reality. Frankly, I'm shocked that the place hasn't surrendered to entropy yet.

The house looks sad, sagging at every window frame. The windows themselves are boarded up, and the black shutters are hanging loose, like dangling teeth. The purple paint on the door is peeling, revealing old, grim-looking bloodred stains. I'm not even sure what color the siding is supposed to be—pink? Purple? A sort of rust-tinged mauve?

I knew I was buying a money pit—and *buying* is, honestly, a wild exaggeration, because the sum total of my new mortgage amounts to a single dollar bill. One dollar… And it's a steal for a dollar, considering the lush half-acre backyard, with a vacant overgrown lot behind it. My sister, who lives with her husband over the border in Toronto, told me about the Home-for-a-Dollar program about a year ago. It's an initiative of Niagara County to encourage homebuyers to fix up houses in depressed areas, thus increasing the overall neighborhood appeal. I'd laughed about the idea—at first. I've never been a domestic, put-down-roots sort of person, and I've taken pride in the fact that, despite my thirty-six years on the planet, I've yet to possess my own permanent address.

But the more I thought about it, the more I realized that this housing program could be my next grand adventure. After years in the field, I craved a pause, a break—and it had to be a *working* break, because I can't stand sitting still, sipping margaritas on a beach or watching television marathons. I really wish I *could* relax like a normal person, but my brain's too frenetic: I'm hoping to fix up this place and flip it for a big profit within a couple of weeks. Or, given my utter lack of carpentry and electric and plumbing skills...maybe it'll take a few months. Six months, tops. And after that... Well, I'll worry about *after that* later. It's my personal policy to put off worrying until the last possible moment—or, hell, just avoid it altogether.

"Ms. Dark?"

"Hmm?" Startled from my thoughts, I turn around, brows narrowed, to face a harried-looking woman wearing an ankle-length skirt and a wrinkled blouse beneath a long knitted sweater. A battered briefcase swings in her grasp as she walks toward me, taking long, quick steps. Her gray hair is drawn up into a messy topknot, and there's a ketchup-colored stain on her collar. But her smile is effortlessly warm and genuine. I return it, reaching out to take her hand.

"Hi. I'm guessing you're from Rainbow Realty—"

"Yes, yes, Ms. Dark. My name is Marie Rosenfeld—please, call me Marie—and I'm so sorry that I'm late. There was a pileup on Robert Moses, and it took ages to sort it all out. I counted six police cars and two fire trucks, but no ambulances, thank the Goddess. I *always* try to be early to my appointments, I promise you, but sometimes, well, fate intervenes." She pauses to shove a loose gray lock behind her ear, clear blue eyes shining above the rim of her wire-frame glasses. "So, how was your flight?"

"Miserable," I say, smiling softly.

"Lots of turbulence?"

"No, I get motion sickness—"

"Oh, my son has the same problem! Since he was a wee one. Now he's grown with a son of his own, and Robbie Jr. can't set foot on a plane without wetting himself and losing his lunch. Like father, like son, I guess. They have to sedate the poor boy whenever they fly out to visit relatives in Reno. Of course, I've suggested more homeopathic remedies—flower essences, healing crystals—but Robbie is a nonbeliever. Anyway, have you been inside yet?"

"Inside?" I glance at the front door of the house with trepidation. Somehow, in the fading afternoon light, the shadowed entrance looks even less friendly than it did only a moment ago. "I haven't gone inside there, no. I just got here—"

"Good!" She claps her hands together with a sharp smack, causing my eyes to widen in surprise. "Then I haven't kept you waiting for long. I do want this to be a pleasant experience for you, Ms. Dark. And given the, well…" Her head tilts toward the house slightly, and she purses her lips, suddenly serious. "Given the *fixer-upper* state of your new home, I want to make this transaction as easy for you as possible. So." She reaches out to pat my hand, as if in sympathy. "Shall we step over the threshold together, hmm?"

What an odd way for a real estate agent to speak, to behave… Of course, Marie looks more like a medium at a psychic fair than a real estate agent, and I have to admit: her hesitant assessment of the house as a "fixer-upper" gave me a strange, unsettled feeling in the pit of my already unsettled stomach.

I regard the peeling purple door again, wondering what hazards lie behind it. Holes in the floorboards, holes in the ceilings? Moldy, mildewy, musty rooms that haven't been occupied by anything other than moths and mice for decades?

Unaccountably, the barista's story of a ghost drifting over the staircase enters my mind—but then I roll my eyes and shake my head, annoyed at myself. What I told the green-haired coffee slinger was true: I *don't* believe in ghosts. Or witches or vampires or zombies. Or reanimated mummies, for God's sake. I believe in the stuff I can see with my own eyes, touch with my own hands. I've never allowed the rampant legends of spooky voices or ancient curses to scare me away from dig sites, so a kid's (probably inebriated) "ghost" experience—while trespassing, no less—rates pretty low on my mental list of Things to Take Seriously.

Sighing, I offer Marie a small smile and step onto the groaning front porch. "Let's check this out."

"All right. You first, homeowner. But please watch your step."

The realty office had sent the door key to my site address in Cairo. After an absurd amount of digging around, I find the key ring in my bag and push the small silver key into the lock. I'd expected some resistance; this door probably hasn't been opened often in the past couple of years. But, surprisingly, the knob turns with little effort, and the bond between the door frame and the door breaks soundlessly, without a single creepy creak.

*Well, that's promising...*

But then I step forward, and my foot gives way beneath me, sinking far lower than the level of the floor. I catch myself on a tall, hard object—a side table? It's too hazy and dusty to see clearly—and manage to avoid falling headfirst onto the hardwood. But my ankle, caught in a hole, twists beneath me.

"Oh, Ms. Dark! Are you hurt?"

"No. It's nothing," I lie, grunting and lowering myself to the floor. I remove my foot from the small gap in the floorboards and sit with my head pressed against my knees, wincing from the hot sear of pain. I'd injured the same ankle in Cairo last week by tripping—weirdly enough—over a black cat that had wandered into my open-air living quarters. *Guess you're in for some bad luck*, Lucia, the site manager, had told me teasingly, after I limped out of my shelter in search of ice. Lucia didn't believe in ghosts or superstitions any more than I did. The locals we hired to help us with the dig had insisted that the urn we unearthed from the desert sand, marked all over with red-painted hieroglyphics, was cursed, so Lucia and I had made a game of blaming our stale coffee on this supposed curse—along with the sandstorms, and that horrid infestation of stinging beetles.

Despite the ache in my ankle, the thought of Lucia now—brown-limbed, sharp-tongued, graceful Lucia—sends a flash of heat through me; I bite my lip, remembering the way she felt in my arms. She and I had shared work and meals and private jokes, and we'd shared a bed, too—sometimes mine, sometimes hers. One night, we made love beneath the stars, a few yards away from the excavation site, our entwined shapes lost in the shadows of a red-gold dune. Her skin was sand and velvet against my tongue...

She's still camped out in Cairo; when she kissed me good-bye, she said that she would write to me here. But I don't expect her to. We're too alike: she, like me, lives a life without commitment. By next month, she'll be off to Greece or South America, where she'll seek out new wonders and warm someone else's cot.

I massage my ankle; it's grown hot to the touch. Frustrated and embarrassed, I smile at Marie self-consciously. "Sorry, I should've looked before I stepped—"

"No, no, *I* should have warned you about that hole. I'd forgotten about it. It's been weeks since I was last here. Things have been so hectic lately, and I wasn't able to come out yesterday like I'd planned to, to do a final walkthrough for you or a sage cleansing. Do you need me to call an ambulance, or drive you to a clinic?"

"I'm fine," I assure her, chuckling softly. "I have a habit of falling. Don't give it another thought." In the dim, slanting light, alive with floating dust motes, I notice a tear on the thigh of my jeans—and then I feel the prick of an upside-down nail beneath me. I must have sliced the denim when I slid down to the floor...

God, I hope the airline finds my luggage soon. In my tacky neon shirt, torn jeans, and coffee-stained boots, I hardly feel fit to be seen by make-believe ghosts, let alone living, breathing people. I rake a hand through my short mess of brown curls and then heft myself to my feet, suppressing a groan.

"Sure you're all right?"

"I'm sure, thanks. I just need to walk it off."

"Ms. Dark—"

"Alex."

"Oh. Alex." Marie's round face looks strange,

almost vaporous, in the angled, dusty beams of light seeping through cracks in the boarded-up windows. "If you don't mind me asking, where are you from? You have a sort of accent, and my father was born in England—London, actually—so I wondered if you might be from England, too. Or Scotland?"

"No." I chuckle again. "I'm not from England. I'm not from anywhere. I've spent some time in England. Boarding school for a couple of years. But I've lived all over. My mother and sister and I traveled with my dad to most of his dig sites while I was growing up, and I kept up the wandering habit after he passed on. I was born in Toronto, though. My sister lives there now. She and her husband have a contracting business."

"Ah, so you're Canadian?"

"Technically speaking, yeah." I smile again. "I haven't stepped foot on Canadian soil in years, though. And this is my first time in the States in about a decade."

"Have you been to the falls before?"

I nod, rising to my feet with a slight wobble and reaching out to the side table again for balance. "My parents used to bring us to Niagara Falls every summer. My dad worked the whole time—speaking engagements at museums and colleges, and he attended the annual conference on archaeology held at the convention center in Buffalo—so my mom and sister Cordelia and I took in the tourist traps without him." I gaze toward one of the dirty-paned windows, its glass boarded over on the exterior of the house. "It was a special place to us," I say softly, trailing a finger over the dust on the tabletop. "We moved from apartment to apartment, from country to country, but always came back to

Niagara Falls in June."

"And now you've come to stay."

My eyes widen, and my mouth, all of the sudden, goes dry. I wipe my sweaty palms on my jeans. "To stay? No, I— No." *Now you've come to stay...* Marie's statement rattles me more than it should. I turn to face her, shaking my head, brown curls drifting in front of my eyes. "Sorry. I haven't come to stay, only to fix up this place and then sell it for a profit. I'll go back to digging. I'm only taking a break—"

"Well, then I hope it's a restful break. I hope it proves to be exactly what you need, Ms. Dark. Er, Alex." With deep calm shimmering in her too-blue eyes, Marie takes both of my hands and squeezes them gently. "I believe that everything happens for a reason. If you feel that you need to be here right now, then you *do* need to be here—and all the rest will fall into place."

I smile slightly, unused to this sort of New Agey talk but oddly reassured by it. Maybe I just feel soothed by Marie's comfortable presence. She reminds me a little of a professor I was fond of during my undergrad days at NYU. "No matter what happens," I say, glancing up at the chipped ceiling with its bulb-less chandelier, and then staring at the curving, purportedly haunted staircase at the back of the entryway, "it's sure to be an adventure."

Marie slides her arm through mine and pats my hand again. "Come on, Alex. Let's begin the tour, hmm?"

I learn, as we walk through the house, that there are eight large rooms in various states of disrepair, in addition to an unfinished basement and an attic. Downstairs, Marie shows me a kitchen devoid of appliances and countertops but with a large, cozy-looking fireplace set into the inner wall; a sitting room with a built-in reading bench beneath the boarded-up bow window; a dining room, square, red, and very dark; and a "salon," as Marie calls the living room, wallpapered in an odd pattern that looks, to my eye, like interlocking fish bones.

Though the rooms are spacious and will probably be bright enough once the boards are removed from the windows, they're in neglected, shabby shape. The place hasn't been inhabited in decades—I'm unclear as to when the last resident vacated the premises—so I had expected grime, but I'm half-afraid of falling through the floors or getting crushed beneath rubble, should the ceilings above my head suddenly give way.

I take some comfort in the fact that Cordelia will be arriving the day after tomorrow to help me assess all of the construction work that needs to be done. Judging by my uninformed first impressions, though, this house should be rebuilt from the ground up.

I hope I haven't made a terrible mistake…

The sinking feeling in my stomach—on top of the lingering post-flight nausea—tells me that, yeah, I probably have.

Well, it won't be the first time a hotheaded decision got me into a jam—and, I'm sure, it won't be the last time, either.

"Be careful on this staircase," Marie tells me, as she stands on the bottom landing, her beringed hand resting lightly on the knobbed newel post. "It's safe enough, but I've fallen on it both of the two times that I've been here. I...um...just felt dizzy all of the sudden and slipped." She glances at me self-consciously; then she shrugs. "Maybe I got lightheaded from breathing in this dusty air. I've had asthma since age three, so that's likely it. Although I should say..." She shakes her head. "Anyway, watch your step."

Following Marie's lead, I take each stair one at a time, admiring the scrollwork on the carved banister as I glide my left hand along it. The faces of the steps themselves are adorned with curlicues and fleur-de-lis, and the wood is stained a rich, dark red-brown. When I lift my head at the first landing, my eyes confront a five-foot-tall stained glass window with a pointed, arching crown.

I pause in front of it, a little stunned, my eyes still as I hold my breath.

I've never seen a window like this one before.

My family didn't attend church services—my father was an avowed atheist, and my mother followed an eclectic spiritual path—but we toured many of the gothic churches of Europe with their soaring architecture and artful, Christian-themed stained glass windows.

This stained glass window, though, doesn't depict a religious scene—no saints or angels or grapes, no crosses or trumpets twined with lilies.

I stare into the glass gaze of a brown-eyed woman, dressed smartly in a black corseted Victorian dress, and I feel something within me, something new or long-buried, move, or quake, or suddenly wake up from a deep, dark sleep. It's the same feeling that I get when I'm trying to remember something and *almost* have it—it's right there at the edge of my consciousness—but I can't bring the memory fully to mind.

Staring at the glass woman, I shiver slightly; the

air feels cold all around me, and the hairs on my arms are standing on end.

"Who—" I begin, but Marie is already nodding her gray head, pointing at the window and looking poised to tell me a tale.

"This house was built by the Patton family," she says quietly, meeting my eye as she clasps her hands over her stomach. "Have you heard of the Pattons? I'm sure you have. They made quite a name for themselves."

"No, I…" I begin to shake my head, but then I pause, thinking. "Patton… You don't mean—are they related to the Patton Papers empire?"

To my surprise, Marie nods her head, smiling her friendly, encouraging smile. "That's right. Godrick Patton dabbled in everything from music to medicine to mummy-collecting in Egypt, but he made his fortune by mass-producing stationery and Valentines for Victorian ladies during the late 1800s. Of course, now Patton Papers is a multibillion-dollar company with no ties to the original Patton family at all. In fact, there aren't any Pattons left alive. At least, not as far as I know." She shifts her gaze to the entryway below us. "But during the heyday of his paper fortune, Godrick Patton built this house. Chose every wood stain and wallpaper—even drew up the architectural plans himself. He was quite the renaissance man."

"Really?" Amazed, I turn again toward the woman's likeness pieced out in cut pieces of colored glass. Somehow, the window artist managed to convey an expression of impishness in the young woman's face. Her eyes are warm but also teasing, and her mouth curves up into a knowing half-smile. Her dress drapes loosely around her small breasts and soft hips, the "fabric" falling to her ankles and concealing all but the tips of her sharp red boots. *Odd,* I think, *red boots, not black.* Her gloved hands hold a piece of paper—a letter, maybe. She's the picture of a wise, worldly woman playing a game, playing her part, in order to get what she really wants out of life. I wonder what she wanted.

"Was this Godrick Patton's wife?"

"No. That's his daughter Elizabeth. Bess, they called her. Godrick's wife Amelia died shortly after Elizabeth was born. Amelia never lived in this house. And Bess was their only child, the only heir."

"Elizabeth," I whisper, biting my lip. A quick, icy chill rushes over me, and I shiver again, even though none of the windows nearby are open. Besides, no cold air could be seeping in from outdoors: the temperature is in the high 70s today, not cool at all. I rub my arms and clear my throat. "So, her father commissioned an artist to make this window?"

"Yes. Godrick loved Elizabeth very much. You know," Marie begins in an odd tone, eyeing me thoughtfully with her head tilted to one side, "you resemble her. Her hair is longer, of course, and you don't seem the type to wear a corset—"

"I'm not," I laugh.

"But there's a resemblance—in the eyes, I think." She nods her gray head, thoroughly convinced. "You both have that look about you, like you're plotting something, or keeping a secret. Oh, and I mean that in the most complimentary way, Ms. Dark. Sorry. Alex. As you can see, Elizabeth Patton was a beautiful girl. Tragic, what happened to her, poor thing." Marie sighs shortly; then she turns on the landing to brave the second flight of stairs. "But enough ancient history. Come along now, before the sun sets. This house is frightfully dark at night, and the electricity isn't on yet. I hope you brought candles."

I didn't, and I'm beginning to realize just how unprepared I am for this harebrained venture. I don't even have a sleeping bag to sleep in tonight, since the airline misplaced all of my luggage.

Marie pauses in front of a pair of open double doors near the top of the stairs. "Now, here's the master bedroom. This was Godrick's room, of course, and I would think it gets the most light—or will, once you pry those awful boards away."

I poke my head into the room but don't step inside; there isn't much to see, anyway. It's a large room, larger than any bedroom I've ever had before, and its wallpaper is a dull gray, though there's the ghost of a pattern of silhouettes. A toile pattern, I think it once was. The room could easily accommodate a king-sized bed, a couple of regal wardrobes, and a full-sized sofa. Marie shows me the comparatively small, empty closet and then leads me onward to the next bedroom, opening the crystal-knobbed door wide.

"You might use this room as an office," Marie says, stepping over the threshold, kitten heels clicking. "It's the smallest of the three. Godrick's mother lived here. She was an invalid and never went downstairs."

"Never? You mean…"

Marie frowns, gesturing toward a darker rectangle on the hardwood floor, where a bed likely stood. "She died in this room, and others died within these walls, too. Elizabeth, for one—"

"Elizabeth? How did she—"

"—but you'll find that's often the case with old houses. It isn't out of the ordinary at all. My own house was built much later, in the 1920s, and there were three deaths beneath the roof before my husband and I moved in." She offers me a soft, sympathetic smile. "We haven't had any *ghost* sightings, if that's what you're worried about, so I...expect you won't run into any haunting activity here." She pauses, gazing toward the ceiling. "Most likely."

"Right," I murmur, even as, against my will, the image of the ghost on the stairs floats up behind my mind's eye. Now its face is that of an old woman, and its hands—reaching, reaching—are faintly wrinkled, creased with long, branching blue veins...

But then the face changes, smooths; the silhouette straightens, reshapes itself into soft, young, black-clad curves, and Elizabeth Patton hovers, translucent, holding out her mysterious letter to me...

Damn that barista and his squatting friend.

The last thing I need right now is to be worried about specters haunting my staircase. Drawing in a deep breath, I peek into the old woman's room, giving it a cursory inspection. It only has one small window cut into the back wall, but Marie's right: this would make a good study. It's gloomy and narrow, and I prefer to work in small, dark places. It helps me focus. I took to writing field reports in caves during an excavation on Mytilene, and ever since then, I've sought out similar spots whenever I need to set down words.

"And now—here's a bit of a surprise for you," Marie says enigmatically, opening the third door lining the dim hallway. "Elizabeth's room, and it's still furnished—can you believe it? Partially, anyway. I'm afraid that the mice and moths got at the linens. Honestly, it's very lucky that vandals never took to graffitiing this place and stealing what was left behind. You could sell this furniture for a high price, I'd think.

It's in good condition, considering its age. Might cover some of the renovation costs."

I blink, nodding my head vaguely as I step into the room and approach the wide vanity pushed against the west wall. The mirror above it is scratched; it has that spooky, aged look that old mirrors get when they aren't properly cared for. But its center is unmarred, so it's still able to reflect an eerie impression of my face: my eyes look too wide: dark, haunted pools of brown inset into the pale planes above my cheekbones, and my hair is a wild mess of slept-on curls. "God, I look terrible," I murmur, in a voice too low for Marie to hear. All at once, that chill rushes over me again—not quite a gust, but there is movement to the air.

"Did you feel that?" I ask Marie, turning around to face her with my brows narrowed, shivering as goosebumps rise up all over my arms. "A cold wind... What could cause it?" I glance up at the ceiling, searching for gaps. "Do you think there's a problem with the roof?"

"Well, the roof does need to be replaced. That's for certain." She takes a step toward me. "Did you feel the wind over there? I didn't feel anything here..." Her voice trails off, as if a thought has occurred to her, but then she purses her lips. "You could bring in an inspector," she suggests quietly, averting her blue gaze, "to prioritize the house repairs and get some financial quotes. I have phone numbers—"

"No, thanks." I shake my head and sigh heavily, already weighed down by the renovation in store for me. I've never owned a home before; I don't even know how to use a lawnmower. And while I'm eager to learn new skills and collect new experiences,

I'm beginning to feel awfully nostalgic for my simple life in that makeshift tent.

"I've got help on the way." I cross my arms at my waist, offering Marie a small, uncertain smile. "My sister's going to drive into town and tell me how to make this place livable. She's a pro at house flipping...though I don't think she's ever attempted to flip a house like *this*."

"It will be a challenge," Marie agrees, returning my smile with her warm, grandmotherly one. "But you seem a capable woman, Alex. You'll turn this sad old place into a home. I'm sure of it. And it's about time. No one's lived here since the Pattons—"

"Wait—what?"

"Oh. Oh, I'm sorry. I thought you'd been told by the agency. Wasn't it in the paperwork that we sent you? *Unoccupied since original residency*? I guess I never said..." She nods her head, peering at me over her glasses. "Well, it's true. The house has been under various ownerships—all acquired through inheritance—and some of those owners did make small attempts at upkeep. Rewiring the Victorian electricity, for example, and updating the plumbing. That's the only reason the place hasn't fallen to the ground yet. But no one actually went so far as to live here. The house has been vacant of life since 1901."

I stare at her, stunned. "But...why?"

"Why?" She shrugs. "I couldn't guess. The property fell into the city's hands after decades of unpaid taxes mounted up. All I know is that no one has expressed any interest in occupying the house, not in over a hundred years. Not until you," she says softly, meaningfully. "Who knows? Maybe, after you finish the renovations, you'll reconsider staying in the area—"

"Oh, no." My chest flutters anxiously at the suggestion, but, if I'm honest, I'm also a little annoyed. My sister has been hinting at the same idea for weeks now: that *maybe* I won't want to sell the place after I've spent so much time renovating it. *Maybe* I'll decide to make Niagara Falls my first permanent hometown.

I know that the only reason Cordelia told me about this Home-for-a-Dollar program was so that she could, in her underhanded but well-meaning way, persuade me to give the picket-fence life a go. And even though, during our last Skype conversation, I made it crystal clear to her that I had no such intention, that I was only taking a very temporary break from work, she had responded with that knowing, big-sister nod that only ever means one thing: *I am older and wiser than you, Alexandra, and I'll humor you, but eventually you'll realize that I'm right. I'm* always *right.*

That nod was the equivalent of a condescending pat-pat on the head.

And Marie is giving me the very same sort of nod right now.

"I appreciate the vote of confidence," I tell her, sighing, "but I'm just not the type of person to *stay* anywhere."

"Mm." She lifts a brow sagely. "Well, time will tell. A fellow said the same thing to me once. Swore he could never put down roots, could never tie himself to a wife and kids." Marie holds up her left hand and points to the twinkling diamond ring on her second finger. It's the least flashy jewel among her collection of rings; the other bands shine with red, purple and faceted turquoise. "But Henry's lived here in Niagara Falls for thirty-two years now, and we've been married for thirty-one."

I bite my lip. "That's wonderful. I'm glad you're happy here, but I—"

"Never say never," Marie says softly, still smiling that patient smile. "This place..." She gestures at the walls around us. "This *town*... It gets under your skin. I dream of the falls every night, you know. I dream of tossing myself over the water in a barrel—a barrel! And I survive! Oh, I don't look like myself at all, of course. I'm a man with a bushy black mustache... Isn't that funny?" Her clear blue eyes connect with mine, liquid, bright and searching. "Have you ever had a dream like that? Where you're someone else, or living in the past? Sometimes I think dreams are kind of like time travel machines, if we only open ourselves up to them."

I smile noncommittally, admiring the unusual seashell—no, ammonite—pattern carved into the headboard of the bed. The truth is, I rarely remember my dreams. When I do, they're meaningless reenactments of daily life, nothing interesting.

"Oh, sorry, we aren't here to talk about me, are we? I have a tendency to ramble; all of my friends tell me so. I was at a séance last Thursday and—oh, there I go again. And I haven't shown you the powder room yet. It's extraordinary, really. This way, at the end of the hall."

I watch as Marie moves out of Elizabeth's bedroom, but I'm reluctant to leave the space myself. It's the only room in this big, crumbling house that feels comfortable—almost safe—to me. The fact that it is the only one with furniture probably has something to do with that feeling. There are even some pictures hanging on the wall: two small, framed sketches affixed right next to the bed. Both of them feature a woman with long, loose hair; she's dressed in Victorian garb and standing with her back to the Bridal Veil Falls. She looks paler, sadder than the woman from the stained glass window. Maybe this was Elizabeth's mother, or a cousin or a friend.

Curious, I test the old mattress with the heel of my hand, leaning forward with all of my weight. It creaks on its support ropes but holds its shape well enough. I might be able to sleep here tonight.

I wish I could sleep right *now*…

"Alex?"

"Sorry. I'm coming." As I step away from the bed and near the vanity mirror again, an unexpected flash—no, a reflection—catches my eye. I could have sworn… I thought I saw a shock of black hair, a pair of black eyes. But it isn't possible. It *isn't* possible. I'm exhausted and ill, and this house is swarming with dust. I did *not* just see someone's profile gliding past that scratched-up mirror's surface.

I couldn't have… *Couldn't* have.

No, I didn't see anything. Maybe I saw a moth fluttering, or a reflection of the curtains on the window—except that…there aren't any curtains. Well, then I've been disturbed by Marie's talk of ghosts and death more than I realized, and my brain is too tired to differentiate between reality and imagination.

Again, I look longingly at the bare bed with its strange, puffy-looking mattress. But Marie calls out— "Is anything wrong?"—and so I move across the complaining floorboards to step into the hallway.

"Nothing's wrong. Sorry. I'm a little slow today."

"Come, come. You'll have all the time you want to linger later. But this room is worth seeing in what remains of the daylight. You'll be pleasantly surprised, I promise you."

Intrigued, I follow her into a large, bright, high-ceilinged space that, at first, appears to be wallpapered with a shimmery seashell pattern. But closer inspection reveals that the walls are covered with *real* shells, and fossils and crystals, too, thousands of them inlaid like tile, with faint traces of yellowing grout in between. I trail a hand over the cool, ridged surface of one of the shells, marveling. "This must have taken ages to complete."

"Godrick and Bess collected all of the shells themselves, on their travels. According to their biographers, they were both fascinated by the natural world."

"Biographers?"

"Oh, yes, there have been several books written about the Patton family. Godrick made a hobby of archaeology, and Bess accompanied him to most of his sites. She knelt down in the sand right beside him, digging with a special trowel. You can see one of her finds on the top floor of the library downtown—a small urn from…Macedonia, I think." Marie pauses to gaze at me thoughtfully. "To be honest, I thought that was your main compulsion for buying this place. The archaeology connection."

"I…didn't know," I tell her truthfully, as I peer at the imprint of an ancient fish on a piece of slate. I feel a little unsettled by "the archaeology connection," to be honest. Modern female archaeologists are rare enough, but a *Victorian* female archaeologist… The odds of my occupying the same house as someone like Elizabeth—without actively seeking to do so—seem astronomical. It's coincidental, too, that Elizabeth became involved in archaeology in the same way that I did, through a father's influence.

"I didn't know anything about this place, or the Pattons," I say, narrowing my brows and shaking my head. "I just liked the photos of the exterior, what I could see of it. The pictures were taken from above and from so far away."

"Yes, we hire one of the helicopter pilots who flies tourists over the falls to photograph"—she hesitates over the word again—"fixer-uppers like this. For most buyers, it's more about the property than the house itself, so the aerial view makes the most sense. And, of course, nearly all of our buyers choose to walk through the houses before making their final purchase decisions."

My mouth slides into a sheepish half-smile. "Guess I'm a leap before I look sort of person." I stare at a large conch shell resting on the floor, next to the clawfoot tub. Idly, I pick it up—it's heavier than I had expected—and turn it over in my hands, admiring its creamy shade. "And things have worked out well enough for me so far."

Marie puts a hand, heavy with jewelry, on my shoulder. "I'm sure this house will be no exception, Alex."

"Thank you. I'm...feeling out of my league. You know, I've never been inside a Home Depot before."

"Well..." She laughs. "You'll be a regular soon enough."

We explore the rest of the bathroom—or "powder room," as Marie keeps calling it—and I'm astonished but deeply relieved to find out that the plumbing in the house does, indeed, work. Marie turns on the hot water faucet for the shell-shaped pedestal sink to demonstrate this to me. I hold my fingers under the stream of water: ice cold.

"No hot water heater?"

"No central heat, either. But if you clean up the chimneys, you'll have working fireplaces in most of the rooms."

My dream of a long, hot, relaxing shower fizzles and fades, but it was an unrealistic expectation. The house doesn't have a shower, only the tub. I can't remember the last time I soaked in a bath...

In Cairo, we all shared an outdoor shower that was superficially private: a thin, almost see-through curtain draped around the round metal rod. Lucia and I had sex today—or...yesterday?—right before I left, in that cozy, open-air shower. We ran out of hot water long before we ran out of steam, and when we came out, sheathed in towels, we were both chilled, shivering. Lucia's lips were faintly blue. I kissed them, to warm them up... And then we realized that half of the crew was watching us, alternately clapping and whistling, as they went about their normal routines.

I guess everyone knew that Lucia and I were sleeping together. We never made a secret of it, but we didn't flaunt it, either. Lucia was uncomfortable with public displays of affection, though she was *unrestrainedly* comfortable when it came to private displays.

I tilt my head thoughtfully. It's strange: I just arrived in the States today, but I'm already thinking of Cairo, of Lucia, in the past tense.

"So, Alex, do you have any questions?" Marie asks me, as we leave the bathroom and step back out into the darkened hall, aiming for the staircase.

"Oh—are you leaving? What about the basement and the attic?"

She turns slightly, offering me a pained smile. "The basement is very dark, even during the daytime, and I'm not certain whether the attic is sturdy enough to support our combined weight. Feel free to explore them as you'd like. But we had better take care of the last of the paperwork downstairs."

In the entryway, Marie opens her briefcase and spreads out some documents on the side table, the same table that had broken my clumsy fall—and the only piece of furniture in all of the rooms downstairs. After she explains the ins and outs of the contracts to me, I sign my name on the pieces of paper, feeling, with the inking of each signature, an unexpected excitement welling up inside of my chest. I caught a case of cold feet as we wandered through the house, as I took in all of the dust and century-old decay, but the idea that, with the simple scratch of a pen, this piece of history will belong to me… There's something exhilarating about that. I've never really owned *anything* before, aside from my excavation tools; some practical, excessively pocketed khakis; hiking boots; and a small collection of paperback novels—mysteries, mostly, and some lesbian pulp fiction books, for the laughs.

Despite the darkness and my exhaustion, I have a sudden compulsion to explore every nook and cranny of this place. I want to pry loose its secrets. I want to find out everything I can about the house's former occupants. I want to unearth every story… I'll have to go to the library tomorrow to look up those biographies Marie mentioned, and to see Elizabeth's urn.

"Well, I think the legalities are in order. You'll receive copies in the mail in a day or two." Marie gathers up the paperwork and then shuts it inside of her battered briefcase—after removing a brown paper-wrapped package. "Just a small housewarming gift from the office," she says, handing the package to me. Then she gives me a beaming, cheek-to-cheek smile. "Congratulations, Alex! You're a homeowner."

"Wow." I chuckle lightly. "Those are words I never thought I'd hear," I say, smiling, dazed. "Thank you for all of your help, Marie."

"Of course. It's been a pleasure passing the hour with you." She opens the front door and steps out into the twilit evening. The dusky sky casts a lavender sheen onto her gray hair. She takes my hand one last time, squeezing it with firm but gentle pressure. Her bracelets tinkle together on her wrist. "If you have any problems, just give me a ring. I'm not the sort of agent to sell a client a house and then disappear. I'm here for you, okay? I know it's tough starting over in a new place—and, in your case, a whole new country. I can get you in touch with folks to help make this transition a smooth one for you."

"I appreciate that. Have a good night."

"You, too, Alex." She clips toward the sidewalk and raises her arm in farewell before hurrying toward her car, a yellow station wagon parked down the street. I get the sneaking suspicion, from her cautious but frantic movements, that this isn't the sort of neighborhood you want to linger alone in after dark. So I'm a little perturbed to note, after I shut the door, effectively closing myself inside of my new house by myself for the first time, that there isn't a deadbolt on the door frame, only a doorknob lock.

First thing to add to my Home Depot shopping list, I guess. Along with a hot water heater.

For a moment, I stand still and bemused in the center of the entryway, staring up at the temple-like ceiling that was once, Marie informed me, covered in gold leaf. Now its color could best be described as filthy, and the chandelier hanging above my head is home to an active community of spiders. Sticky gray webs dangle from every branch of the tarnished light fixture. It would be a nice effect if, say, this were a haunted house attraction. Convincingly authentic. And creepy. But since I'm not planning on billing the place as Alex Dark's Haunted Victorian Adventure, I should probably add a ladder and a heavy-duty duster to my mental shopping list, too.

I draw in a deep breath, trying to calm my hamster-wheel mind. There's a hush of expectancy in the air. I'm not used to this sort of quiet: an indoor quiet, accompanied by the faint swish of car tires on the street outside, of distant voices rising and falling in laughter, or anger, or fear. I feel closed off and, at the same time, exposed. I almost feel…as if I'm being watched.

*Paranoia, really?* Further proof of my need for sleep.

I rake a hand through my hair—or try to; my fingers get caught in a snarl—and then I pull out my cell phone from my back pocket. There are three unread texts: two from Cordelia and one from Lucia. I decide to read Cordelia's first.

*r u there yet? send me pictures alexandra! i want house porn! c u in 2 days!*

Then, in another text sent twenty-five minutes later:

*hey is it all right if I bring jack to nf with me? david just got a big job and will b out of town. love u!*

I bite my lip thoughtfully. Jack is Cordelia and David's five-year-old son. I've never met him, only chatted with him on the phone and on Skype, but Cordelia likes to claim that he takes after me: he's curious, unruly, and prone to getting himself into trouble. He also inherited my rat's nest head of hair, poor kid.

Jack ran away from home when he was three years old to "find treasure like Auntie Alex." His three-year-old definition of treasure: an old soda can that he dug up from the side of a highway. Half an hour after he went missing, Cordelia and David found him wandering beside the road with his sand shovel, looking very serious as, crouching, he poked at the ground.

*It's too dark for pictures. You'll see the house for yourself soon enough. And I'd love to meet Alex, Jr. Bring him along,* I text Cordelia, smiling softly to myself. My sister and I talk often, but we haven't been face to face in years. She's my best friend, the only person I've ever truly confided in. I've missed being in her warm, familiar—if mischievous—presence. Cordelia pretends that she's the responsible sister, but the truth is that she's just as unconventional as I am. She hides her quirks better than I do, though.

I tuck the phone back into my pocket. I'll save Lucia's text for later...

As I ascend the staircase, Elizabeth Patton's glass eyes follow me—teasing me, or challenging me; it's impossible to tell which. *Who are you?* I ask her silently, pausing before the window and resting a hand

upon her cool, alabaster cheek. She doesn't answer—
of *course* she doesn't answer—and, with a sigh, I turn
my back to her and set off for the bathroom.

The hallway is so dark now that I trip over a
loose floorboard and nearly knock my head into a wall.
Luckily, there's a sconce in the way, so I scrape my
cheek against cold metal, instead, nearly dropping
Marie's package to the floor. A moment later, I feel a
warm trickle of blood on my face.

"You didn't see that, did you?" I ask Elizabeth-
in-the-window, as I press my fingers to my cheek. My
nails come away stained with red. "Normally I'm as
graceful as a swan, I swear."

*Nice, Alex. Lying to the girl already…*

Sighing, I rip the package open and am pleased
to find a new set of bed sheets—Egyptian cotton with a
high thread count. The thought of sleeping on a naked
Victorian mattress was, admittedly, kind of unappealing.
So I spread the sheets on the bed and then stumble into
the bathroom, closing the door behind me. There are
two large windows, side by side, set into the back
wall—impractical for privacy purposes, but useful now.
These windows, maybe because they're at the rear of
the house, aren't boarded up, so some rosy light
illuminates the seashell-encrusted walls—and allows me
to find the toilet without further injuring my body or
my pride.

I pee in the old-fashioned toilet gingerly. When
it comes time to pull the cord, I hold my breath, hoping
that the contraption will actually flush. It does, though
the sounds it makes in the process are jarring, bone-
rattling, actually frightening. If I were a little girl, I'd
imagine, based on those sounds, that there was a
monster in the pipes. But since I haven't been a little

girl in a very, very long time, I imagine a massive plumbing bill, instead, and feel the beginnings of a migraine behind my left temple.

I wash my hands and inspect my face in the mirror. The cut from the sconce is small, an inch-long diagonal gash, but it's still bleeding. I don't have anything to clean it with or to press against it, except...

I shrug out of my hideous t-shirt and use it to apply pressure to my face. As I stare at my half-naked reflection in the mirror, I realize that I've just bloodied my one and only wearable shirt; I haven't even got on a bra. The top that I wore on the plane is in a plastic bag in my purse, but it's encrusted with desert sand and hours' worth of nausea-induced sweat. I'd opt for the bloody Niagara Falls t-shirt before I'd put that thing on again.

I take stock of the situation. The airline promised they'd deliver my luggage tomorrow. I might have to answer the door topless, but it wouldn't be the first time I've done such a thing—or even the second time. Or, well, the third. I'm not really shy.

Once my face has stopped oozing blood, I drop the t-shirt and remove the cell phone from my back pocket; then I kick off my jeans and panties and leave them in an untidy pile on the bathroom floor. I'm about to leave the bathroom when something trembles in my peripheral vision. Something—I realize, dry-mouthed—in the mirror.

I'm no longer standing in front of the mirror, so I couldn't have seen my reflection. But when I stare into the aged silver glass, there's nothing there, only a backwards image of the bathroom wall. Am I so tired that I've begun to hallucinate?

I shake my head, trying to shake loose my

rationality.

I step out into the hallway and stand in front of Elizabeth's room, and that cold feeling envelops me again. This time, goosebumps rise up all over my body; I wrap my hands around my arms, chilled to the bone.

It must be the roof, letting drafts into the house... Cordelia will know how to fix that, surely. She's installed hundreds of roofs, thousands of roofs. Patience has never been my strong suit, but I've just got to put up with this hair-standing-on-end feeling for one more day. One day. No big deal.

The enthusiasm I'd experienced just before Marie left to launch an exploratory expedition inside of the house has, with each moment's passing, slowly dissolved. All that remains now is an overwhelming desire for sleep. I move into Elizabeth's bedroom, past the vanity, and I lie down, full-length, upon the mattress that, I can only assume, Elizabeth once lied upon herself. She must have had a fabric canopy, but now there are only gray rags hanging from the posters. I had a canopy bed, too, growing up. It was the one "girly" concession that I made—but only because the fabric draping all around me made me feel as if I were in a secret clubhouse, or a cave, or in a cabin on a ship. Or cozy in a tent in a wide, vast sea of sand...

Propping myself up on my elbow, I read Lucia's text on my phone:

*I'm thinking of you, A, & touching myself for you. Touch yourself for me. Pretend my ghost is there beside you, watching you. God, we had some hot times, didn't we? Jojo keeps teasing me about the shower. I'm heading off to Mexico City soon. If you're around, lmk. Hate to think I'll never taste you again. XOXO*

I groan and lick my lips, tossing my phone onto the floor with a clatter as I roll onto my back. The darkness is more or less complete now, but I close my eyes, anyway, summoning Lucia's strong brown body, envisioning her hands…as my own fingers tease at my nipples, already hard from the cold. I pinch them, just like Lucia pinched them: until they hurt, until I cried out but never, ever asked her to stop. I never wanted her to stop… If she were here, her wet mouth would move from my mouth to trail hard, possessive kisses over my chest, my stomach, my upper thighs. Lucia was neither a gentle nor a hesitant lover. Now she would claim my stinging center, her breath like licks of fire against me; my fingers move to that ache now, imitating the rhythms of her tongue…

It doesn't take long—it never took long with Lucia—before the white-hot wave rushes through me from my head to my toes, and I sink into that blissful, time-stopped feeling, where all I know is this sensation, this invincibility and fragility and, finally, this soul-deep, natural calm…a calm I never feel in any other context. I've sought it out in every corner of the world—on islands where there was nothing but ocean for miles; in temples, where peace was palpable in the air—but I'm only truly easeful, relaxed, after a violent crash of ecstasy.

When I've caught my breath, I fetch my phone from the floor and send Lucia a quick text:

*I felt you here tonight. Hard to believe there's an ocean between us. But, hey, we'll always have Cairo. (Sorry, you hate that movie.) If I'm ever near Mexico City, you'll be the first to know. XXX*

Sighing, I curl onto my side, feeling oddly lonely. Odd because I'm rarely lonely. That's why fieldwork has been ideal: the isolated landscapes, the solitary work, being hundreds or thousands of miles apart from the people I love... I don't mind it. I like the freedom. I like the hunt, just as my father did. Mom always said that he and I were born "searchers." The truth is, though, that Cordelia is as addicted to mysteries as I am. She just indulges that longing by reading Agatha Christies and solving more practical quandaries, like The Case of the Leaky Pipes and The Mystery of the Creaking Front Door.

Maybe the sadness of this house is getting to me. Godrick's mother died here. According to Marie, Elizabeth died here, too. Who knows what other tragedies took place between these walls before it lay forgotten, before it sat vacant, save for some squatting insects and—judging by that skittering I just heard in the closet—mice?

I don't believe in ghosts, but I do believe that sadness leaves a mark. It's certainly left its mark on me.

Just before I drift off to sleep, I glance toward the mirror and see an impossible thing: an orb of light, about six inches wide, floating in front of the glass. Startled, I sit up, but the translucent ball vanishes just as quickly as it appeared, darting through the open door, out into the hallway. I shake my head, gripping my aching temples in my hands, too tired to wonder, to think.

A bug. It was probably a bug. Or the headlights of a passing car.

I fall back onto the mattress and dream of dunes, and Lucia, and the woman in the sketches by the bed, reaching her arms out to me... She says something, again and again, but I can't hear her over the roar of Niagara Falls.

# Chapter Two

"All right, Ms. Dark." The young woman reaches across the large mahogany desk to hand me a laminated card. "Your paperwork checked out, so here's your new library card. If you have any questions about our collection, just pay a visit to Trudy over there at the Reference Desk. And welcome to Niagara Falls! It's a great place to live."

"Thanks," I smile, tucking the card into my pants pocket.

The airline was true to its word; my missing luggage arrived at the house at seven-thirty this morning, and I accepted the delivery without ever coming out from behind the front door. The deliveryman could clearly tell that I was naked—his pale, stubbled face flushed a deep red once he took in my bare arm and the not-so-hidden curve of my hip— but he was professional about it, averting his eyes and allowing me to sign his clipboard without ever compromising my—or, more likely, *his*—modesty.

It feels glorious to be wearing my own clean clothes again. I'm far from prissy; I lost any prissiness I had when I was a little girl, accompanying my father on his down-and-dirty, one-shower-a-week-if-you're-lucky digs. So this morning I gave myself an icy sponge bath using one of the hand towels in my suitcase, tied up my disastrous hair with a plaid bandanna, and strode out of the house in my favorite khakis and a soft white button-up shirt.

In the daylight, my neighborhood looked shabby but hopeful. There's a new apartment complex rising up one block over, and I took note of several promising prospects for pizza and Chinese food delivery. Signs affixed to the telephone poles advertised everything from Neighborhood Watch groups to yard sales, book club meetings and dog-walking services. Granted, there were a few too many police cars cruising Cascade for my comfort, but the street was quiet enough—and almost pretty, with its autumnal trees nearly at peak.

It's strange: my spirits are pretty high, despite the cold, pathetic night I passed, plagued by dreams rife with loss and longing. I can hardly remember the dreams now, only the feelings they left behind, but there is one image that still lingers: the woman from the sketches on Elizabeth's wall, gesturing to me in front of the falls. Weird that I would dream of her and not Elizabeth herself, after all of my wonderings.

To jump-start my sleep-addled brain, I braved the retro grooviness of Bean Power, and I have to admit, I'm growing fond of the mud-puddly Desert Siesta brew.

Now, standing in the center of the high-ceilinged, spacious library, I turn around to search out the aforementioned Trudy, of Reference Desk infamy. For some reason, I expected her to look like a '60s-era school secretary, with a black beehive and thick glasses swinging on a long chain around her neck. But the reality of Trudy couldn't be further removed. I trip on the leg of one of the study tables when she notices me and, brow arched, meets my deer-in-the-headlights gaze.

"May I help you?" Her voice is husky, her red-lipsticked half-smile sly. She props up her head on her hand, blonde waves spilling down to the desk, as her blue-violet eyes brazenly scan my length, taking in my coffee-stained boots, my messy curls—and, lingeringly, everything in between.

"Ah, new in town?" she asks, quirking her mouth up at one corner. "You must be. I'd have remembered seeing you before."

"Yeah, I just arrived yesterday," I tell her, feeling absurdly tall; she's still seated, so I have no choice but to loom. "Um, I was wondering if you could—"

"—go out with you tonight? Sure, I'd love to." She winks, twirling a black pen in her right hand as she swings her desk chair to the side, baring her short-skirted legs to me—along with her dangerously spiked sky-blue heels. "Where should I meet you?"

"Wow. That was—"

"Quick? I know. I'm not into wasting time with all of that *is she or isn't she* stuff. I mean, you *are*, aren't you?"

"Well, yeah—"

"And I am, too. And you're hot, and I'm pretty sure you think *I'm* hot. Nice save with that table leg, by the way."

I chuckle and bow my head, surprised to realize that I'm blushing. I pride myself on making other women blush…and I'm kind of turned on by the role reversal here. Trudy looks as if she stepped out of a 1920s gangster movie. I've always had this thing for gun molls—sans the guns, of course. "Well… Why not? Okay, sure. There's a coffee shop on Palmer

Street—"

"Bean Power? Tacky as hell. And awesome. Say, 7:00?"

I smile, gazing into her kohl-lined purple eyes. "Seven's my favorite number."

"Mine, too. See, this is fate." Effortlessly, she swings beneath her desk again and lifts up a hardcover book, presenting it to me. "Speaking of fate... My current obsession."

The dust jacket design is alarmingly New Age, with an arcing rainbow superimposed over the photo of a woman gazing off into the middle distance, looking surprised or inspired or, I don't know, Touched by an Angel. I read off the title: *Everything Happens for a Reason.*" Funny... Marie had used that same phrase yesterday, when she was insinuating that I should stay in Niagara Falls for good. Frowning slightly, I hand the book down to Trudy. "Looks, um, uplifting."

"And you look faintly nauseated. Okay, okay, never mind." She puts the book into a drawer in her desk. "It is kind of fluffy bunny, I guess. And you seem like"—she pauses, putting on a deep English accent—"a serious sort." She leans forward, hands beneath her chin, framing her cleavage prettily; her extraordinary eyes latch onto mine. "Let me guess. You enjoy reading dry scientific journals about cutting-edge robotics and giant particle colliders."

My lips curve at her teasing. "Something like that. Actually, I was wondering if you had any biographies about a pair of amateur archaeologists who lived around here during the Victorian era."

"Whoa. Caught me off guard there, I have to admit. Are you a historian?"

I smile. "I'm an archaeologist."

"Ah." Her blue-violet eyes flash appreciatively. "Makes sense. I got an Indiana Jones sort of vibe from you. Okay, give me a sec." Trudy turns toward her flatscreen monitor and starts clicking with the mouse. "Okay, names? Dates?"

I feed her all of the information I have about Godrick and Elizabeth Patton, and after a few minutes of research, she makes quick notes on a slip of white paper. "Looks like we have three biographies about the father, which I would assume include mentions of the daughter. Pity no one's written a biography about her yet, hmm? But isn't that always the way? If you aren't a princess or a movie star, good luck at ever getting your life story in print, ladies. That's why I'm going to write my own autobiography. Anyway, here you go, tiger."

"Alex."

"Hmm?"

My mouth slides into an easy half-smile. "My name's Alex. Alex Dark."

"Oh, my God, Alex *Dark*? You should be a comic book superhero. Are you? Is that how you got that cut on your cheek? Do you save damsels in distress—when you aren't researching obscure historical figures?"

I shake my head, lifting a regretful brow. "Sorry to disappoint you."

"Trust me, Alex Dark." Trudy gives me a long, slow once-over again, cat eyes narrowed, red mouth drawn into a wide, appreciative grin. "I'm *not* disappointed."

I find the Godrick Patton biographies easily enough—they're positioned side by side, between a Louis Pasteur biography and a tell-all about a female pop star that I've never heard of before. Further proof that I'm wildly out of touch with modern American culture. After I peruse the archaeology books, choosing a couple that highlight Western New York-born archaeologists, I limp on my reinjured ankle up to the third floor of the library, where the special Niagara Falls collection is displayed.

The large, open room, spanning the full width of the library building, feels cozy despite its size, illuminated by the warm yellow sunshine streaming through the skylights of the raftered ceiling. I peer into the rows of glass cases, many of them containing old photographs of early Niagara Falls glory: people in Victorian dress gathered on the falls viewing areas, or walking arm in arm downtown. There are postcards and postage stamps, novels and storybooks, newspaper clippings detailing the thrill of hydropower and the tragedy of ill-fated barrel dives. It isn't until I reach the final case—featuring prominent Niagara Falls residents—that I find what I'm looking for: Elizabeth's urn.

Only it isn't an urn; it's a water flask made of rough-hewn pottery, and a beautiful example, dyed saffron with vegetable extracts and inked with a strange, spiraling design. Frankly, I'm surprised that the flask has been archived here, rather than at a museum, but Elizabeth—being an amateur, and a female amateur, at that—didn't have the status of most other archaeologists of her time. It's entirely possible that no one with academic historical or archaeological interest has ever even seen this flask, or heard of its existence.

I lean in closer to read the flask's placard: *Ancient flask, discovered in Macedonia by Elizabeth Patton, daughter of Godrick Patton of Patton Papers. The Pattons built and occupied the house at 1080 Cascade Avenue in Niagara Falls from 1876 to 1901.*

And that's it. That's *it*? Nothing about Elizabeth's globetrotting adventures, or the fact that, as a lady archaeologist—amateur or not—she was a rare creature, at odds with her repressed, patriarchal time?

Maybe I was expecting too much from a display case placard, but I'm insatiably curious about all of this, too hungry for facts, stories... Hopefully the biographies will tell me something of value about Elizabeth, or give me a jumping-off point for beginning my own research.

Disappointed, I let go of the case, leaving finger smudges on the glass, and begin to turn away. But a thick, curling piece of paper positioned just behind the flask catches my eye as I'm about to head off toward the stairs.

I peer down at the little drawing, a rough sketch in pen and ink, and my heart stumbles. *Is it really*...But it is; it's her, the same figure drawn on the sketches hanging by the bed at the house. I'd know her lovely face, her liquid length, anywhere, in any context.

There's a placard positioned by the drawing, too: *Portrait of Victoria Richards inked by Elizabeth Patton.*

Victoria Richards...

The dream comes back to me, comes back with such force that I have to take a step backward and grip my head to combat the sudden dizziness. I see her so clearly, that woman standing with her back to the Bridal Veil Falls. She's dressed all in white, and her hair is as yellow as gold. The contrast between her dress and her hair is stark, disorienting, and when she lifts her arms to me, she opens her palm and reveals something bright, something shining.

Is it a coin? I can't tell—

"Are you all right?"

"What?" I blink my eyes at the elderly man standing just to my left; he's hesitantly touching my elbow, as if to steady me. "Sorry. Yeah. Yeah, I'm okay. I'm just... I was only remembering something."

He nods his head politely and moves off, convinced of my relative sanity—though I have to admit, I'm beginning to doubt it myself. Why did I react like that to an old drawing? It's bizarre... I've rarely felt out of control—save for that Sunday in March, when the accident happened... But that was an extreme circumstance, an anomaly, and there was a clear cause and effect. Here, there's no cause, only a picture, and a vague picture at that. Apparently Elizabeth was something of an Impressionist. Her drawings are clearly of a long-haired woman, but my dream supplied the hair color, the facial features, the graceful limbs and sad, seeking gaze.

*God...* Maybe that Bean Power barista spiked my coffee with a hallucinogenic drug. Or maybe I breathed in too much black mold at my new, incredibly old house. I hope one of those scenarios plays out to be true, because the alternative is that I've gone stark-raving mad. If I can help it, I'd rather not become the bedraggled Miss Havisham on the block, raving about heartache, heartbreak, from decades past.

Feeling shaky but slightly more lucid, I venture near the case again. Who was Victoria to Elizabeth, I wonder? A friend? A fellow archaeologist? Or just a model, not an acquaintance at all? But why would Elizabeth have hung Victoria's portraits by her bedside, if that were the case? No, they must have been close.

Flushed and uneasy, I make my way back downstairs and check out my books at the scanning machine near the Reference Desk. "See you tonight, superhero," Trudy calls out, and I wave to her distractedly as I shove the books into my bag and, foggy-headed, move through the revolving glass door.

"You're late."

"I'm sorry. And I hate to make excuses, but I don't have a clock, and my phone died because I haven't got an adapter or electricity yet—"

"No clock, no power. What kind of slum are you living in?" Trudy teases, nudging the straw of her frothy drink between her pink-glossed lips.

I smile weakly as I take the seat across from her. "A Victorian on Cascade Avenue, actually."

"Cascade..." Her startling blue-violet eyes widen. "You're braver than I am. My friend Cory got jumped on Cascade just last year. It's a rough street, Alex."

"So I've heard." I tilt my chin on my hand, offering up an admiring smile. "You look beautiful."

"You're not so scruffy yourself."

Trudy changed her makeup, and her face looks softer now, younger, too, with pink and violet replacing the harsher red and black. Stripped of eyeliner and that aggressively sexy lipstick, she reminds me of a girl that I dated in undergrad—Sophie Travertina, the blonde English major and wannabe novelist. We broke up when we realized that, after being exclusive for four months, neither of us had any desire to move in together. To this day, I've never lived with a romantic partner, and, given my propensity for travel, I doubt that I'll ever share a roof—except, maybe, with a dog. I've always wanted a dog.

"Can I buy you a drink? Something to"— Trudy's eyes take me in, loitering at the thick leather belt at my waist, and then sliding a little bit lower, her lips parting, tongue flicking over her too-white teeth— "*energize* you for the wild night of passion to come?"

Surprised, I laugh softly. "Is that the plan?"

"Mm. Let's be straight, all right?" She shoves her half-full glass off to the side and takes my hands; her wide mouth slants into a lopsided grin. "Not *straight*, obviously, but…honest. Honesty is my policy. So…I'm kind of a free spirit. I like to keep all of my doors open, you know? I think you and I have a little spark between us, and I'd like to see that spark become a great big lightning bolt…" She trails her long, lavender nails over my palms; I lick my lips and suppress a shiver. "But I'm not really into monogamy. I mean, it's cool and all, and maybe someday I'll settle down with the proverbial *woman of my dreams*, but right now, I'm just looking for something casual." Her mouth slides up at the corners. "And sexy. And since you seem both casual *and* sexy—"

"Thanks, I guess…"

"What do you say? How's about you whisk me off to your little love nest on dirty old Cascade?"

"Well…" Chuckling, I still her ticklish fingers and entwine them with my own. Her nails poke into my skin softly, and I realize that it's been a long time since I dated a woman with long nails; archaeologists tend to keep their nails short and unpainted.

"It could be dangerous, you know," I whisper playfully, gazing into Trudy's bright, eager eyes. "Not only because of Cascade's reputation, but… The truth is…I think my house—or *love nest*—is haunted."

Her jaw drops, and she pulls her hands out of mine to lay them flat on the table, nearly tipping over her drink. "Ghosts? Honest-to-goodness *ghosts*? Oh, this is perfect! I'm an amateur ghost hunter."

"Really?" I laugh.

"Mm. And I've never had sex in a haunted house before. That could be kind of creepy…" She touches a finger to her chin and regards me with a wicked gleam. "Good thing I'm into creepy stuff. Let's go!"

"What—now?" I laugh and lift my brows as she rises from the table, straightening her short, clingy black skirt. "But we haven't talked. You haven't told me anything about yourself." I fall back against my chair and stare up at her, amused by her pouty, impatient expression. "Come on. I don't even know your last name."

Trudy leans over me then, so that her half-bared breasts are—quite purposefully—within my line of sight, and she positions her face, her mouth, very near to mine. My eyes flick over her features; my body warms at her closeness and begins to arc toward her. She smells of old paper and cotton candy. "Guess what?" she says. "I've got a superhero name, too: Trudy Strange."

My eyes widen. "Really?"

"Really." She snakes her hand into mine and, before I can protest, neatly pulls me to my feet, drawing me tight against her, her free arm clutching at my waist.

"So what do you say—up for a Dark and Strange time, Alex?"

I bite my lip and feel my mouth move into a slow smile. "Always, Trudy."

"That's what I like to hear. Then come on, tiger. Let's fly."

⋅◈⋅

Trudy pins me against the front door as soon I shut it behind us, her mouth hot and hungry against mine, her body soft and warm as it molds itself to me; I break the kiss and moan as she moves her bare knee between my legs, applying pressure there—gentle at first, but then harder, faster. With one hand, I unhook her bra, digging my nails into the smooth skin of her curving back.

"Bed?" she breathes into my ear, kissing the line of my neck and sliding her hand beneath my shirt.

"Oh, well…it hasn't got any pillows," I pant, pausing to claim her mouth, savoring the sugary flavor of her lip gloss, "and it's old and might not be up for all of this…Darkness and Strangeness…" I grin against the kiss.

"Well, what the hell! Who needs a bed, anyway?" Trudy declares, and with that, she's pushed me down to the dusty floor, right over the wretched hole that tripped me up yesterday, and somehow she's already unbuckled my belt and unzipped my fly. With expert fingers, she shimmies my pants over the length of my legs, and I kick off my boots, laughing.

"You weren't kidding when you said you don't like to waste time," I whisper into her ear as she bends over me, wavy blonde hair trailing over my collarbones.

She ducks her head for a long, deep kiss that steals my breath from my lungs and makes my heart pound like a drum. "Coincidentally…" I begin, "I don't like to waste time, either."

Grinning, I wrap my arms around her waist and roll until I'm lying on top of her, my hips pressing hard against her hips, my mouth at her neck, tasting her salty-sweet skin—

"Should've guessed you'd play dirty," she laughs, arching her back as my kisses move from her throat to her chest, and then to the soft, pink curves of the tops of her breasts. She moans beneath me. I slide my fingers under her shirt and bra, then, and she tosses the clothes off to the side, pulling my hair, pulling me close. Again, her knee angles itself between my legs.

With a groan, I fall upon her large, lovely breasts; I suck at her nipples, teasing them, biting them, and as she begins to thrust her knee harder against me, I slip a hand under the waistband of her skirt, of her lacy panties, searching for her wetness—and then I massage her as I lift my head, crashing my mouth against her cotton-candy lips.

For long moments, minutes, we hold that kiss, still touching, moaning, pressing our bodies close together, tormenting one another in small, practiced, delicious ways.

"Oh, God, Alex," Trudy gasps for air, long nails scratching at the fabric on my back; clawing, desperate, those nails slip beneath the hem of my shirt, trailing ticklish paths over my sides.

Catching her hands and pinning them down beside her head, I made a tsk-tsk sound, leaning over to kiss her mouth so hard that our teeth clack together. "No distractions while I'm working," I breathe against her; then I leave her mouth and lick her hot length. Her skin flushes a shadowy scarlet. I bite her nipples, pinch them with my fingertips as my lips travel lower, lower, tongue teasing at the edge of her skirt.

"Alex…"

I rise up onto my knees and straddle her; my hands slide between her skin and her skirt and drag the bunched black fabric down, over her hips and legs, revealing a pair of black panties embroidered with the words MISS STRANGE.

"Are all of your clothes personalized?" I ask, smiling, edging my fingers beneath the beribboned elastic band.

"Most of them. I never said I wasn't vain. Besides, every girl needs some luxury in her life— oh…ohhh…yes…tiger…"

Trudy's panties now lying beside her other clothes on the floor, I smooth my hands over her bared legs, gliding my tongue along the inner curve of her thigh…

"Yes…please…"

…and then I'm tasting her at last, as her hips begin to buck around me. I give myself over to the bliss of her, the sweet scent of her, and when she grows quiet, eyelids closed upon her pink cheeks, I slide my fingers inside of her, gently rotating my fingertips as my tongue continues its slow, wet ministrations.

Her hips thrust upward then—once, twice, three times—and I feel her thrumming, squeezing, hear her crying out as the orgasm moves through her; her hands seek my hair and pull hard, tangling in the curls. A minute passes, two, as she relaxes, lets go of my hair, drawing in slow, trembling breaths, eyes still closed.

Finally, she laughs a hoarse, raw laugh and tugs

at my hair again, pulling me on top of her, neatly rolling me over, just as I had done to her. "Your turn," she says—or tries to say, but the words scarcely leave her tongue before she gasps, falling to the side of me and gaping toward the staircase. "Alex, there's…there's…"

"What is it?" I smile lazily up at her, grazing her folded leg with my fingertips. I shiver slightly, suddenly chilled, despite the heat and longing still raging through me; the outdoor temperature must have dropped. There are goosebumps all over my skin, and, I notice, all over Trudy's skin, too.

"No—*look.*"

"Trudy, what's wrong?" I take in her expression—shock, or, no…fear—and sit up quickly, placing a hand on her shoulder, turning to follow her line of sight.

It must be after eight o'clock; the downstairs windows are still boarded up, save for the small window in the door, and there aren't any lights on, no candles, nothing; visibility fades in the recesses of the entryway, and the stairs themselves are awash with strange, multicolored darkness, thanks to starlight or streetlights beaming through the stained glass window of Elizabeth Patton. Trudy's attention wasn't caught by the quality of light there, though, but by the *being* of light adrift on the steps, descending in eerie, slow, floating degrees.

"There's a g-ghost," she finally manages to whisper, sliding nearer to me, wrapping a cool, shaky arm around my waist. "You were serious. I thought you were *j-joking.* Your house is *haunted.* Oh, my God, I just orgasmed in a haunted house. Alex." Her grasp on my waist tightens. "Is it friendly, like Casper?"

"I don't…" I stare in mute astonishment at the illuminated shape. At first, it looks like a vaguely person-shaped mass of gray light, hazy, undulating with shadows. But as I stare, that shape begins to take on distinction, features—there, the curve of a hip. And there, I think, is the long, flowing hem of a gown. It's a woman; it *feels* like a woman, like a female's gaze, pointed toward us, somehow serene in its unhurried drifting and its silence.

"Alex!"

"I—I'm sorry," I stammer, reaching for her hand and giving it a weak squeeze. My muscles feel oddly liquid, and my heart is beating so quickly that it seems as if it isn't beating at all. "I've never seen…that…before. I—someone told me a story, but—"

"Should we go?" Trudy whispers urgently, pressing her chin to my shoulder. "Do you think it'll hurt us, *possess* us or—"

"No. No, I don't think it will."

"How can you be sure?"

I shake my head. "I'm *not* sure." I swallow and lick my dry lips. I want to look away, look at Trudy, comfort her, kiss her again, ignore the impossible specter looming behind us.

But I'm unable to remove my eyes from the apparition on the stairs. Though it had appeared to be descending at first, I realize now that it's lingering halfway down the staircase: its loose skirt sweeps around its feet, as if caught in a breeze, creating the illusion of forward movement. The skirt is dark; the whole body is dark, save for the too-white arms and face and the smooth, shadowy updo of its hair.

As I watch, in one strange sweep of its head, it looks to the left, over the banister and into midair, presenting us with a clear view of its profile.

Elizabeth Patton. It looks like Elizabeth Patton, the woman in the window.

I blink, shaking.

Honestly, I think I'm in shock.

"Oh!" Trudy says then. "It's fading, I think."

But the ghost doesn't fade so much as evaporate, separating into infinitesimal pinpoints of light, like a Seurat painting, or like the clouds of mist generated by Niagara Falls. "Water dust," my mother always called that mist, as if the falls were engaged in a never-ending spree of hydropowered Earth-cleaning.

My mouth hangs open as the phantom—a gathering of pulsating dots now—drifts upward, disappearing moments before it touches the ceiling. There's an odd *whoosh* to the air around us when it goes at last, icy and quick but somehow soundless.

"It's gone." Trudy's words, whispered against my neck, hang heavily in the dark, empty space around us.

"Yeah," I say, "she's gone. It's okay. We're okay. She's gone." There's no question that she's gone. We saw the ghost vanish, but the house *feels* different now, too. Vacant. I couldn't have described it before, but now that I've had the experience and can make a comparison, I realize that there was a being-watched feeling just before the apparition appeared, an instinctive awareness of a presence in the house other than Trudy and myself.

The cold air has given way, too, to a more comfortable evening coolness. I stare in wonder as the hairs on my arms begin to settle back into place.

For a long moment, we sit quietly together, breathing hard and fast as our bodies begin to warm again, as the chills gradually alter to fever, to flushed excitement. I stare at Trudy; her blue-violet eyes are as wide as my own eyes feel, and her lips are softly parted, as if she wants to say something but can't quite summon the words, or a voice.

I gather her into my arms, sighing out. "Are you all right?"

"Yeah. I'm...freaked out but okay. I think. How about you?"

"Same." I laugh, drawing back to make a joke about voyeuristic ghosts, to try to lighten the mood and chase off my own unsettled feeling, but my eyes fall to Trudy's kiss-swollen lips, and before I have a moment to pause, to think, I'm kissing her again, and she's kissing me back, with twice as much fervor as before. She pushes me down to the floor and snakes her naked leg between my knees. She makes short work of my shirt, grabbing it by the collars and tearing it open with a little growl. Buttons scatter over the floorboards, pinging against the cracked wood trim.

"Easy there, Miss Strange," I grin, reaching down to tease her with my fingers.

"Sorry. I guess ghosts really turn me on." She bites my nipples as she moves against my fingers, lips sliding into a sexy sideways smile. "You know," she says, lifting her head to regard me impishly, "I think I've just acquired a new fetish."

I push my fingers deeply into her as her fingers begin to slide over my own hot, aching wetness. I moan and half-laugh, full of adrenaline, short of breath. "Haunted sex?"

"Mm. I could try it in cemeteries, and abandoned buildings, and—oh...oh-h-h," she moans. "Okay, enough talking. Time for Miss Strange to give Miss Dark some strange, dark lovin'. Up for it, superhero?"

But she doesn't allow me a chance to respond: her mouth locks onto mine in a hard, breath-stealing kiss, and all thoughts of the ghost on the staircase drift out of my mind, as easily as a gust of wind moves through an open window—and then, just like that, ceases to exist.

# Chapter Three

My eyes skim over the two-columned list for the third time, and for the third time, I groan and clutch at my hair, shaking my throbbing head. I didn't get much sleep last night; I tossed and turned on my blanketless bed, and my restless thoughts kept cycling through the memory of Trudy lying naked beneath me—superimposed with the sight of the dimly glowing ghost who interrupted our kisses, the ghost who apparently resides in my house.

It's crazy, surreal. I don't believe in ghosts— *didn't* believe in ghosts. But now…I don't know what to believe. I don't know what to do. I've never had a living roommate, much less a see-through, floating-over-the-stairs, disappearing-into-thin-air roommate.

I had hoped my sister's arrival and assessment of the house's renovation requirements would give me something to focus on, a more-than-welcome distraction from paranormal concerns. But the list of repairs she handed me five minutes ago made my blood pressure rise for a new, all-too-mundane reason.

"Cord, are you sure we have to—"

Cordelia holds up a silencing hand, her long red nails looking wildly out of place against the backdrop of her paint-spattered denim overalls. "Alex, come on. I've known you your whole life. I changed your diapers, taught you to drive a stick. Do you trust me or not?"

"I trust you, but—"

"Look." She reaches for my hand and tugs me over to the staircase, pushing me down until I'm seated on one of the bottom steps. My skin prickles at the sensation of sitting here, where the ghost hovered, phantom skirts billowing around her phantom legs, but I clear my throat and bite my lip as Cordelia squeezes beside me and gives me a gentle but pointed stare. "I crossed the border to help you, all right? I'm not going to leave you high and dry in this big old dust-and-mildew factory. I'll repair everything for you that I can, teach you how to use some sexy power tools, and I'll help you find professionals to take care of the rest of it. This old lady'll be restored to her Victorian glory before you know it. Have faith!"

I nod my head vaguely, slumping against the wall. "I'm sorry. I'm just…feeling overwhelmed. But I appreciate the help, Cord." I smile into her warm green eyes. "You know you're my favorite big sister."

"I'm your *only* big sister, you jerk." She punches me playfully in the arm, and I pretend to be mortally wounded. As usual, she rolls her eyes at my less-than-convincing dramatics. "Anyway," she says, gesturing to the list, now folded, in my hands, "the work that has to be done may look monumental on paper, but in reality…" She pauses to consider. "It's only massive. Colossal at worst."

"I'm pretty sure colossal is bigger than monumental."

"Hey, which one of us has a Master's degree in English, hmm? For all the good it did me," she mutters, mouth slanting into a rueful smile. After graduating from college, Cordelia had intended to get a job at one of the big publishing houses in New York. But then she met David Lavalier at a mutual friend's party, and before long, they were picking out silverware patterns and launching a successful husband-and-wife contracting company. Cord jokes about the romantic, shoebox apartment lifestyle she might have led in the big city, but in truth, I've never seen her happier than when she's on the job. She has a natural knack for building and design, and—like me, like Dad—she loves getting her hands dirty.

"Don't question my words," she says, with a faux-arrogant flourish of her hand, putting on a nose-in-the-air, snooty tone of voice, "and I won't question your…digging for treasure, or whatever it is that you do on those silly little vacations of yours."

Smirking, I reach an arm behind her back and tug on her long brown braid. "I really missed you, you know."

She bumps against my shoulder, bowing her head. "Missed you, too, world traveler. I still find it kind of hard to believe that you've bought a house—"

"To sell," I add quickly. "I bought a house to fix up and sell. Not to stay. I'm not—"

"I know, I know. I wasn't accusing you of *settling down*, God forbid. As she has told me, oh, nine thousand and seventeen times, Alexandra Dark is *incapable* of settling down."

"Stop teasing," I smile softly, lowering my gaze. "Anyway, I haven't made a name for myself yet. I haven't found my holy grail. So I'm not done," I wink at her, bumping her shoulder again, "digging for treasure. Maybe someday, when I'm as old as this house and content with my contribution to the annals of archaeology, I'll…" My grin widens; I glance sideways at my blatantly skeptical sister.

"Right. And maybe someday I'll fly in a rocket ship to the moon. Who are you kidding? You'll breathe your last breath in the desert, and they'll have to pry your quote-unquote holy grail out of your cold, dead hands."

"Probably," I laugh, shoving off from the step and offering Cordelia a hand as she begins to stand up, brushing dust from the seat of her overalls. "So, where has that rugrat of yours run off to?"

"Oh, knowing him, he's probably leapt over Niagara Falls—twice—by now."

But when we find him in the backyard, Jack is quite innocently squatting on the overgrown, browning grass, watching a green dragonfly flit over the wildflowers. He has a little notebook on his lap, and it looks as if he's been trying to draw the dragonfly with his number two pencil; unfortunately, I think he's inherited the Dark family's artistic talent—or lack thereof. His dragonfly looks a bit like a sausage wearing an overcoat.

"Jack, darling, tell your Auntie Alex what you got up to yesterday. I'm sure she'll be interested to hear all about your adventure." Cord turns toward me with an arched brow. "When Jack realized that we were coming to visit you, he wanted to find you a present."

"Not a *present*, Mum, a *treasure*. I almost caught it, but then it slipped out of my hands. Next time I'll catch it," he says, and begins working at his drawing again.

Glancing to Cord, I see her mouth the word *snake*; she shivers, making a disgusted face. Cordelia's always had a fear of snakes. Weirdly, though, she's fond of spiders and had a pet tarantula when she was in eleventh grade.

I laugh softly. Then I lower myself beside the sandy-haired boy, hands on my knees, and nod toward his drawing. "Is that your field notebook there?"

His eyes—the same green-gold eyes that his mother has, that I have, that my mother had—light up behind his glasses, as if a switch has been flipped. "I draw bugs in it, and sometimes fish. We went to the aquarium and..." Dropping the pencil to the ground, he begins flipping through the notebook's pages. "Here it is! Look!" He presents me with a scrawl that might be a crab, or a hand, or a tree. "I saw an octopus!"

"Oh, how exciting," I smile at him, regarding the drawing with interest. Well, he drew eleven tentacles and colored the flesh with scribbles of yellow-green crayon, but I guess the sketchy creature does resemble an octopus, now that I have some context. "You know, I kept a notebook just like this when I was a little girl."

"I know. Mummy told me."

I peer over my shoulder at Cordelia; she's beaming down at the two of us with an expression that can only be described as glowing. "Look at you guys, like peas in a pod." She sniffles a little, quickly swipes at the corner of her eye. "It's just... I've waited five years for this moment. I'm so happy that you're here, Alex," she says, adding quickly, "even if it's only for a temporary stay."

"I'm happy I'm here, too," I tell her, standing up to wrap my arms around her in a long, tight hug. Her hair smells of wood dust, along with a faint hint of jasmine perfume—our mother's perfume, I realize. Drawing back, I smile at my sister and my nephew, feeling more content than I have in a very long time. "What do you say we take this junior explorer out for lunch somewhere? I don't know about you guys, but I'm starved."

Jack springs to his feet, the notebook falling from his lap to the grass, abandoned just like his pencil. "Could I have macaroni and cheese?" he asks, looking hopeful in the bare, wholehearted way that only a child really can. "And chicken nuggets?"

"Of course, kiddo." I ruffle his hair, resting a hand on his shoulder. "I don't exactly have a kitchen, and I haven't checked out the local eateries yet, but I'm sure we can track down some mac 'n' cheese for you. Ready to go, sis?"

Cord smiles at me, nodding her head as she begins to aim for the house. "Let me make myself presentable. Be back out in a minute. You two get better acquainted while I'm gone—and stay away from that pond, young man," she calls, as the back door closes behind her with a sharp-sounding click.

I shift my gaze toward the vacant lot adjacent to my backyard. There are small orange flags separating the two spaces, but no fence, nothing to keep Jack out should he become curious enough to explore. The pond Cordelia mentioned, roughly the size of a hotel pool, is near the back of the property. Dragonflies skim its surprisingly clear surface, and cattails line its muddy bank.

Jack falls down to the ground again, scooping up his notebook and pencil, peering all around—up, down, left, right—as if he's determined to find something, anything, worthy of a sketch.

I sit down cross-legged beside him, idly pulling up bits of dead grass.

I've never been comfortable with children, have never, for a moment, wanted any children of my own, but I've adored Jack Lavalier since I saw his first photograph, taken at the hospital right after his birth. I'd sent Cord a Turkish blanket and some yellow booties as gifts, and tiny, red-faced Jack was wearing both the blanket and the booties in the picture. His eyes were wide open: he looked half-fascinated, half-shocked. Something happened in my chest when I looked into his newborn eyes, and that same something is happening right now, as I watch Jack's five-year-old hand clutching at the pencil, making clumsy lines on the wrinkled white page.

I draw in a breath to ask him about his adventures, to ask him to describe the treasures he's unearthed in Toronto, his hometown, but he pauses in his sketching and looks at me with such eerie, unexpected intelligence that I close my mouth and tilt my head at him, waiting, curious, for him to speak.

But once he does speak, I wish I had interrupted him and veered his train of thought in another direction. Because, in his little-boy voice, he very earnestly tells me, "Auntie Alex, there's a ghost in your house," and then returns to his sketch of a desiccated leaf.

I remain still, watching him, unable to summon a response or even move, though my neck muscles have begun to ache. *Auntie Alex, there's a ghost in your house.* I haven't told Cordelia about what happened last night—and, to be honest, I never intended to. Though she's practical-minded and, for the most part, very down to earth, she has always had a passing interest in paranormal novels and somehow acquired a Ouija board when we were growing up—until our mother found it and made her throw it out with the trash. If I mentioned the staircase sighting to her, she'd be too eager, too excited; she'd want to explore every nook for more unexplained activity. She'd want to buy another Ouija board to contact the ghost and learn its history.

I only want it to go away.

Its presence makes me uneasy. It makes me doubt...everything. It makes me wonder if I know anything for certain at all.

Biting my lip, I still Jack's drawing hand with my fingers; he glances up at me, surprised, and says, "Don't be afraid."

"What?" I feel my skin grow clammy, and my heart skips a beat. "I'm not... I'm not afraid."

"She won't hurt you, Auntie Alex."

"Who won't hurt me?" I whisper, shaking my head. I try to swallow, but my throat is too dry.

Jack's attention returns to his notebook. He draws some jagged lines on the leaf that I assume to be veins, sighing softly. "Bess," he says, as if that were obvious, as if I should have known, and then asks, "Can I get a milkshake, too, Auntie Alex? Chocolate. Chocolate's my favorite."

❧ ⟡ ☙

Yawning, I tug at one side of the comforter as Cordelia tugs at the other, pulling it taut across the inflated air mattress. It's nearly midnight, and it's been a long, full day of restaurants, shopping, and playgrounds, capped off by a brilliant display of fireworks over Niagara Falls. Jack is already fast asleep, curled up like a baby fox in his Batman sleeping bag spread out on the floor.

I sit down on the cushy air mattress with a sigh, smoothing my hand over the velvety soft beige blanket. We stopped at Target in the afternoon to stock up on essentials—toilet paper, a mop, a broom, feather dusters, liquid cleaners, laundry detergent, flashlights and batteries, gummy worms (for Jack), and warm flannel sheets and faux down blankets. The comforter on my own bed is striped, gray and black.

Despite its small size, Cordelia chose the bedroom next to mine as sleeping quarters for herself and Jack, rather than the big master bedroom at the top of the stairs. "This one feels cozier," she said, when she stepped into the room where—according to Marie—Godrick's mother had lived and, unfortunately, died. I didn't mention that to Cordelia. And, as far as I know, Jack hasn't shared his eerie knowledge of the ghost in my house with his mother yet, though I'm bracing myself for the inevitability.

My sister sits down on the mattress beside me, pats my hand, and offers me a tired smile. "Jack loves you," she says quietly, nodding toward her dreaming, messy-haired kid. "I mean, he's always idolized you—his adventurous Auntie Alex—but now that he's met you, I'm afraid he won't ever want to go back to boring old Toronto with me."

"Well," I say, considering, "I could use a pint-sized cohort on my digs, to squeeze into the nooks and crannies I'm too big for." I gaze at him fondly. "I think we'd make a good team."

"You would," Cordelia agrees, chuckling. "But don't suggest it to him. He'll take you seriously. I swear, that kid is five going on thirty. He wants to grow up entirely too fast." She arches a brow at me. "Remind you of someone?"

I widen my eyes in faux innocence.

"Come on, Alex. You were driving Dad's jeep by the time you were eleven. And you were kissing girls in the baseball field dugout before you reached junior high."

"Shows what you know," I laugh. "My first kiss was with Shelby Maxwell in second grade."

"*Second* grade?"

"Mm. She made the first move, actually. Told me she'd trade me her dinosaur sticker for a kiss-on-the-lips-no-spitting. And who am I to turn down a dinosaur sticker? It was holographic." I offer my sister a sly look. "I guess I always have been in kind of a rush to 'grow up.'" I make air quotes with my fingers. "But for his sake, I hope Jack enjoys his childhood while it lasts. It would've probably done me some good to play more."

"Yeah, you never quite got the knack of playing." Cordelia smiles, shaking her head. "You used to build organizer cubes for your rock collection out of your Legos."

I grin. "While you made unicorns and lopsided castles."

"Speaking of lopsided castles..." She nods at the room around us. "We're going to turn this place into a palace, you know."

I shrug noncommittally. "I don't need a palace. Just a house that I can sell."

"Beautiful houses sell faster."

"Well," I smile at her, "you're the expert. My real estate fate is in your hands." I stare at the walls thoughtfully; then Cordelia yawns. I pat her knee, gazing into her sleepy green eyes. "All right. Enough chitchat. See you in the morning, sis."

"Wait."

I start to rise, but Cordelia catches my arm, drawing me back down beside her.

"What—"

"Tell me the truth: are you okay, Alex?" My sister tilts her head, worry creasing her brow.

"Of course I'm okay—"

"No, I mean, are you *really* okay? You can talk to me, you know. When I suggested this whole house-buying venture, I never thought you'd go for it. And when you did...well, I was kind of concerned."

I blink and shake my head. "What do you mean?"

She lowers her gaze and pauses for a moment, as if considering her next words. Then she draws in a deep breath and meets my eyes. "After Mom and Dad's plane crash, we dealt with our grief in different but...kind of similar ways. I buried myself in home renovations, and you buried yourself in the past, stuck your head in the sand. Literally." She smirks softly and squeezes my hand. "We both ran away from the pain. And we've never—we've never really *talked* about what happened, you know? It's this great big monster lurking in the shadows that we've become experts at ignoring. But ignoring the monster doesn't make it go away. And running from it doesn't make the pain disappear."

"No." I exhale heavily through my nose, clasping my hands over my knees. "I don't think the pain will ever disappear."

"But it could become softer, maybe, if we leaned on one another a little more." As if to prove her point, Cordelia leans against my shoulder, offering me a wide, though gentle, smile. "God, I wish I'd been there, you know?  I could've stalled them somehow, or come up with some reason—some elaborate *ruse*—to force them to cancel their flight, and that would have changed everything, would have saved their lives—"

"We can't change the past," I whisper, choking down a half-formed sob.  "If there's one thing I've learned in my line of work, it's that.  What's done is done.  All we can do is learn our lessons from what's happened and move on."

"But we haven't really moved on.  Have we?"

When Cordelia meets my gaze, I see ten years' worth of sorrow shimmering in her bright green eyes. And I know that my eyes are a mirror of hers—same color, same pain.  It's been a decade since the plane that my parents chartered crashed over Peru, but I still remember that day with crystal-clear perfection.  Dad called me in the morning, so excited about taking Mom to Machu Picchu for the first time.  It wasn't a working vacation, just a vacation-vacation, a rarity in my family. "I think this is exactly what she needs," Dad told me; I could hear the hope, the smile in his voice.  Mom had had a difficult couple of months, having lost her own mother to cancer, and Dad thought this trip would lift her spirits, give her an opportunity to feel joy again.

It probably would have, if they'd ever arrived at their destination.  But the plane's engine malfunctioned, and the useless, burning hunk of metal went down in flames.

There are all kinds of hauntings. I've never been able to erase this image from my mind: my parents trapped inside a plummeting, smoking airplane with no chance of survival.  Careening down from the sky.  I see it when I wake in the morning, before I fall asleep at night.  Did my mother scream?  Did my father scream?

Did they hold one another's hands? Did they think about my sister and me?

Were they afraid?

Of course they were afraid.

"Alex."

I taste the tears before I feel them, hot and itchy, on my cheeks. Sighing shakily, I offer my sister a pained smile. "It still hurts as much as ever."

"Yeah. It does." She sniffles and wipes her nose with the back of her hand. "I...I wish they'd gotten the chance to meet my little guy," Cordelia whispers, pointing her chin toward fast-asleep Jack. "They would've loved him. He would've loved *them*. But, you know..." She pauses, chewing on her lip and staring at me before continuing in a low voice, "Sometimes Jack tells me that Dad visits him. Tells him things."

My mouth falls open; I narrow my brows. "What—you mean, in dreams?"

Cord shakes her head. In the dimness of the room, her shining eyes look eerie, too bright, too wide, and a shiver races over my skin. "He swears he's not asleep when it happens. He says Dad appears in his room and tells him that he's happy, that he loves him, that he loves—and I quote—Axle and Crod very much."

My stomach seizes; I gape at my older sister and clutch the sides of the mattress. "No, that's... Come on. He couldn't... He must've heard you mention—"

"I never have, Alex. I never even told *David* what Dad used to call us."

I shake my head in astonishment. "How could he possibly—" I begin, but then I stop myself, remembering, with a chill, the ghost of Elizabeth

Patton floating, cloudlike, on my staircase.

Right.

Contrary to my former convictions, ghosts are—distressingly—real.

Does that mean Jack truly saw my father's ghost?

I feel dizzy, off-balance, as if the floor is shifting beneath us. Given the wretched state of this house, the floor *might* be shifting, but more than likely, I'm just overwhelmed by all of these revisions to my worldview.

The thing is, Dad loved anagrams; he used them all the time, and he made anagrams of my and Cordelia's names—Axle for Alex and Crod for Cord. He rarely called us by our given names. In fact, I worried when he called me *Alex*, because it usually meant he was upset with me, or about to start in on a serious conversation.

He called me *Axle* on the phone the day that he died.

"I know you're a big nonbeliever, Alex," Cordelia says softly, "but I've done a lot of research into the paranormal, and I just don't think Jack's making this up. It isn't only that I *want* it to be true. And, God, you know I want it to be true." She faces me and nods, but then her eyes fix on something far off, and she breathes out a heavy, weary sigh. "It doesn't matter, anyway. We can't bring them back. I...I really wish we could."

"Yeah. Me, too."

We hold onto one another, sobbing quietly, for several moments, and it's strange and comforting at the same time. We never did this before; we never mourned together. The funeral was too hectic and crowded, and afterward, we were too exhausted and depressed to talk.

Now it feels terrible to cry, to remember, to grieve all over again, but it also feels necessary—and long overdue.

Thank God Jack is a heavy sleeper. He never stirs, not even once.

By the time I hug Cordelia good night, my throat is sore, and my eyes are puffy and stinging. I stumble into my bedroom, blinded by tears, too tired to wash my face or change into pajamas. I sit down on the edge of the bed and stare into the vanity mirror. After a long moment, I imagine that I see a face there—a face that isn't mine. A hard face. Angry, scowling. A man...

But when I shake my head and look at the mirror again, my own face gazes back at me, cheeks red-streaked and pale.

I curl up on my side on top of the new striped comforter and fall into a deep, dreamless sleep.

# Chapter Four

Cordelia is as good as her word. Within a week, the house—which we've named Victorianus Rex, V. Rex for short, in honor of the dinosaur weather vane—has a new roof, a fresh coat of mauve exterior paint, shiny kitchen appliances, and a glorious hot water heater. Cordelia also contracted an electrician to take a look at the wiring, and a plumber to inspect the ancient pipes. The boards are gone from the windows, and that transformation alone has made V. Rex feel like a home, with its sun-washed (and freshly polished) staircase and hardwood floors gleaming like tiger's eye.

I dip my paint brush into the can and glide it along the edge of the molding in my bedroom, Elizabeth's old room. The color I chose is the same shade of burgundy red as Elizabeth's boots in the stained glass window. While I'm not *purposefully* trying to appease her ghost, I can't deny that the reality of her presence always hovers at the back of my mind, subtly influencing my choices for the house's decor. I assume that whoever buys this place will be a history buff, anyway, interested in maintaining the period integrity of the building, so I'm opting for some Victorian-style furnishings—antiques and reproductions—to set the stage. I've discovered, unexpectedly, that I kind of enjoy interior decorating. There's really no need for me to decorate a house I'll soon be selling, but it'll be an added incentive for the next homeowner—since I intend to include all of the furnishings in the sale.

Well, obviously.

I won't have much use for a green velvet-upholstered fainting couch on my dig sites. Though, granted, it might come in handy if Lucia and I work on a project together again...

I tilt my brush on the paint can's rim and kneel on the floor, staring at the red-streaked wall. Truth be told, I haven't been thinking about Lucia at all during this past week. And she hasn't sent me any more texts, so I can only assume she hasn't been thinking of me, either.

But I *have* been thinking about another woman—a woman with long yellow hair and an endearing inability to speak about *anything* without resorting to sexual innuendo.

I flick my gaze toward the stack of library books on the top of Elizabeth's vanity. It's been seven days since I met Trudy Strange, and aside from the small matter of the ghost, she's been topmost in my thoughts. Sure, I've tried to distract myself with the renovations, with ordering frou-frou decorative elements from online stores...

But I can't get Ms. Reference Desk—with her haunted house fetish and her embroidered underwear—out of mind. And, honestly, I don't want to.

Cordelia and I have been so busy working on the house, though, that I haven't had time to stop by the library again. I haven't even cracked open the books I borrowed about the Pattons. Every night when I fall into bed, I'm sore, spent, too exhausted to read or even keep my eyes open. I've always admired my big sister, but I have a new-found respect for her line of work and the seemingly endless supply of energy—and enthusiasm—she has for home repair.

Tomorrow Cord and Jack are taking the day off, skipping over the border to spend some time with David, so maybe I'll swing by the library in the morning, see if Trudy's there. She made it pretty clear that she isn't into exclusive relationships, and for all I know, she never dates twice.

But she charmed me, surprised me...

And really, really turned me on.

I've got to give it a try. Worse comes to worst, she'll turn me down, and I'll come home and eat ice cream on my Victorian fainting couch. Maybe the ghost of Elizabeth will take pity on me and haunt the staircase again, just so that I don't feel alone.

I lift my paint-spattered hand, tracing a finger over my lips. I keep reliving Trudy's kisses, hard but so sweet... *She* tasted sweet—

"Auntie Alex?"

"Mm?" Startled, I disrupt the balance of the brush on the paint can, and the bristles smack onto the hardwood floor wetly, leaving behind a blob of dark red that looks a little too much like blood. I frown at the mess but then smile at Jack curiously. "Hey. What's up, my intrepid nephew? Isn't it kind of late for you to be awake?"

"You have to come. You have to come *now*."

"Oh. Okay." Frowning again, I stand up, gazing down at the messy-haired boy. Normally, when he approaches me, he's excited about something, eager to share a new discovery. But now he just looks like a scared kid. "Is something wrong? Where's your mother?"

"Outside. In the backyard. And..." His green eyes are saucer-wide, his cheeks pale as ash. "Someone else is with her."

"What?" A thousand scenarios—each more dire than the last—race through my mind. Everyone warned me that Cascade Avenue was dangerous, but I shrugged their fears away. I never honestly thought...

Without another word, I fly out of the room, down the staircase, and I hurl myself through the back door. A split-second later, I curse myself for not grabbing my phone or a weapon of some sort—but just as quickly, those thoughts are replaced by cold, paralyzed shock.

Because there isn't an armed man standing in my backyard with Cordelia.

There's a ghost.

And...it isn't Elizabeth.

It's the woman from my dream.

I'm acutely aware of the goosebumps on my arms, of the sharp, pointed stars overhead, of the shush of cars on the road in front of the house: the natural contrasting starkly with this floating proof of the *super*natural.

"Alex," Cordelia whispers, though she doesn't look at me. Her eyes are trained on the ghost—a lithe, pale female form wearing what appears to be a long white dress. The ghost's hair, too, is long and white, or colorless. I blink at her, dry-mouthed, frozen in place, remembering how she beseeched me in my dream, her back to the falls, her hand held out, showing me something—

"Alex," Cordelia says again, her voice a frightened whisper, "um...I think your house is haunted."

"I think it is, too.  I mean, I know it is."

"You *know*?  You *knew* it was haunted befo—"

"Sorry.  I should have told you, but—"

"Yeah.  You really *should* have told me."

"But I've never seen *her* before—"

"Her name is Victoria."

"*What?*" Cordelia and I hiss simultaneously, wheeling around to face Jack.  He looks small and uncertain, standing in the doorway behind me, his white face cast in shadows.

"Her name is Victoria," he says again, quieter this time, his narrow shoulders cowering.

"How do you know that, Jack?"  I swallow, staring into his too-wise eyes.

He shrugs, pointing his gaze down to his bare feet.  He's wearing baby blue Spider-man pajamas, which make him look even younger than he really is.  "She told me."

"She told you.  When?"  I shake my head, baffled.  "How?  Where?"

"When I was playing outside today."

"Are you sure?  It wasn't in a dream or—"

"No," he interrupts me vehemently, lifting his green eyes to meet mine.  "Not a dream.  It was *real*, just like when Grandpa comes.  And when Bess comes."

My heart thuds in my chest.  "Bess..."

"Who's Bess?" Cord asks, still fixed in place, still gaping at the ghost.  "Who's *Victoria*?  What the hell is—"

The ghost vanishes.

"—going on?" my sister finishes weakly, blinking at the space the ghost—Victoria—had occupied, now an empty plot of overgrown grass.  For a moment, Cordelia wavers on her feet, shaking her head, silent. And then she says, "I need a drink. And probably some therapy."

"Come on," I sigh, stepping forward stiffly and threading my arm through hers. "Let's go inside, put Jack to bed. Then we'll get hammered, and I'll tell you everything I know."

⋅⋆❦⋆⋅

Two bottles of wine later, Cordelia and I are flushed and drunk—but only fractionally more relaxed. We tucked Jack in right after the ghost disappeared and then stumbled down to the kitchen, one of my favorite rooms in the house now that it's been furnished with modern appliances—including a microwave. I didn't inherit any of my mother's cooking prowess and tend to live on takeout and reheated leftovers. Right now Cord and I are sharing a box of vegetable fried rice, sloppily pinching the rice granules between our trembling chopsticks.

"All right, so we know who Bess—Elizabeth— is, but this Victoria? Where'd she come from?" Cord asks, slurring the words. She downs the rest of her glass of wine and cradles her head on the round, heavy table that we found at a local antique shop. The books I borrowed from the library are scattered between us. We pored through them, searching for any mention of a Victoria, but aside from paragraphs about the English queen—no luck.

"Was she Elizabeth's friend, neighbor?" Cordelia's sleepy eyes lift, and she catches my gaze meaningfully before adding, in a low voice, "Lover?"

I draw in a deep breath and shake my head.

"I'd be lying if I said that thought hadn't occurred to me. But I'm kind of biased...and we don't have proof of anything. All I know is that the placard at the library by Elizabeth's drawing read *Victoria Richards*. And the woman in that drawing is the same woman in the drawings by my bed—Elizabeth's bed." I pause, considering. "You never took Jack to the library here, right?"

Cordelia shakes her head.

"So he couldn't have known the ghost's name was Victoria just by seeing her. She really must have spoken to him, told him who she was. There's some connection between Elizabeth's ghost and Victoria's... There has to be. But what? Do you think Jack might know?"

"I'm almost afraid to ask him." My sister sits up and offers me a tired, watery smile. "For all of my fascination with the paranormal, Alex, I'm kind of freaked out to discover that this stuff is *real*. I mean, I believed Jack had talked with Dad's ghost...but I haven't ever *seen* Dad's ghost. Now that I've seen Victoria— God, it's like I don't know what's real anymore. I don't know if I should be excited or terrified. I don't know what any of it *means*."

"Me, either." I reach out and squeeze Cordelia's hand.

"Like, why did these people become ghosts? Are their spirits unable to find peace? Is *Dad's* spirit unable to find peace? Shouldn't he be with Mom somewhere, drinking scotch on the rocks on a fluffy white cloud?" A single tear leaks out of Cordelia's bright green eye. "Is there no peace for *anyone*?"

"Cord." I squeeze her hand again. "Look, we aren't—I don't know—ghostbusters. Or psychics. Or parapsychologists. We need help. We need to find an expert, someone who can put all of this stuff into perspective."

She laughs softly. "Right. So who you gonna call?"

I return her wry smile, but then, all of the sudden, I remember something Trudy said to me at the coffee shop: *I'm an amateur ghost hunter.* Granted, she may have been kidding. Or exaggerating. Or even showing off. But, hey, it's worth a shot. Plus, this gives me a solid excuse to talk to her again, without coming off as, well, lovesick.

Which, yeah, I kind of am.

God, I had no intention of falling for a woman in Niagara Falls.

Of course, I had no intention of buying a haunted house, either.

Ever since I arrived in town, my life has felt haywire, out of control. Marie from Rainbow Realty tried to convince me that I had come here for a reason, and Trudy, more or less, said the same thing. But is that reason a *good* reason? Was I wrong to take this detour from my rootless life?

To be honest, it doesn't *feel* wrong. In fact, it feels kind of...awesome. I'm an adventurer at heart, and this spectral mystery is hitting all of my treasure-hunting buttons. Like Cordelia said, it's scary and exciting, all at once—and I love that. I just wish it didn't stress me out so much, philosophically speaking. This whole haunting thing has robbed me of my skepticism badge, and I feel like I have to reexamine every conviction I've ever had...

I gather the library books into a pile and stand up, circling the table to help my woozy sister to her feet. "Let's get some sleep, okay? I'm going to give a friend of mine a visit tomorrow, see if she has any ideas about what we should do next. But I want you to promise me that you won't worry about this, that you'll have fun with David and Jack on your day off?"

Wobbling on her legs, Cordelia gives me an unconvincing salute. "I promise. Just...don't get possessed or anything while I'm gone."

I laugh humorlessly. "I'll do my best."

"And have lots of sex with that 'friend' of yours, okay?"

"What? I never said she was *that* kind of friend—"

"Can't pull the wool over these eyes," Cordelia slurs, motioning vaguely to her ears. "I *know* you, little sister. You only use the word *friend* when you really mean *friend with benefits*. Am I right, or am I right?"

"You're right," I smile, slinging her arm over my shoulder. I drank just as much as Cordelia, but I've always been able to hold my liquor better than her. So I hold her up with one arm and carry the library books in the crook of my other elbow. But by the time we reach the top of the staircase, I have to drop the books to the floor, because I'm supporting all of Cordelia's weight.

I deposit her gently on the threshold of her bedroom, but she reaches out for my arm before I turn away.

"Mom always said our family was a little bit psychic, you know." Cord's eyes are liquid green and wide as moons. "Maybe that's why you're here. Maybe those ghosts *summoned* you here, Alex. Maybe they need your help."

"My help? For what? Digging up an ancient

relic? Because that's about as far as my expertise goes."

Cordelia tilts her head to one side and squeezes her eyes shut, as if she's thinking hard. Or suffering from a migraine. Possibly both. "Well," she whispers, meeting my gaze again, "maybe you should just *ask* them what they want. Who knows? They might answer you."

*Ask them what they want...* A cold chill races over my skin, but I shake it off, exhaling a deep breath I hadn't realized I'd been holding. I smooth a tangle back from Cordelia's forehead and then pat her shoulder. "Good night, sis."

"Good night. Don't let the bed-ghosts bite." She laughs as she moves into the room and belly-flops onto her air mattress with a soft thump. I'd forgotten how adorable Cordelia is when she's drunk; she reverts to her five-year-old self. Whereas I just get kind of melancholy and pensive.

I heft the library books up from the landing and then aim for my own half-painted bedroom, where I collapse, with an *oof,* onto the bed. My brain is too full of weird thoughts right now for sleep, so I crack open the first book on the pile and start to read.

*Godrick Patton was a true renaissance man. He excelled as a musician, a physician, an archaeologist and, most famously, as a stationery mogul. But above all else,* the text informs me, *Godrick was a father. He adored his daughter Elizabeth Violet more than anyone else in his wide, rich, limitless world, and the house he built on Cascade Avenue was his love letter to her.*

# Chapter Five

Disappointed to find Trudy's desk vacant—maybe she has the day off—I wander up to the top floor of the library to look at Elizabeth's drawing of Victoria again. There's no one else viewing the Niagara Falls collection, so I have the whole place to myself. As I make my way toward the glass display case, I notice a newspaper lying open on a chair, and one of the headlines catches my eye: *Haunted House or Hoax? The Ghost Team Aims to Find Out.*

The Ghost Team?

I pick up the paper and put my hand over my mouth, stifling a surprised laugh. Because, just above the article, there's a photograph of a group of four people wearing Ghostbusters-style jumpsuits—though, instead of the trademark beige, the jumpsuits are, shockingly, hot pink.

I think I can guess who's responsible for the costume revision...because, smiling brightly and beautifully at the center of the group, her arms draped around the shoulders of her fellow teammates, is Trudy Strange. While everyone else in the photo looks a little uncomfortable and a lot silly, Trudy, unsurprisingly, is just *hot*. Somehow she's styled her jumpsuit to look coy and vintage, with the buttons undone to reveal her cleavage, and the pant legs rolled up to show off her legs and her pink-and-white-striped heels.

Sexy as hell.

"You're drooling."

I feel Trudy's mouth beside my ear, her hot breath against the side of my neck, as her candy-sweet scent wafts all around me. "Can you blame me? You really know how to wear a jumpsuit," I whisper, smiling, without turning around.

She encircles my waist with her bare arm and presses her body against my back. "I'll model it for you sometime. But only if you promise to rip it right off."

I chuckle softly. "Deal."

"Good. Wanna practice now?" Trudy grips my belt loops and whirls me around to face her. I take in her glossy pink lips, her buttercup-yellow '50-style dress, her pineapple-yellow hair drawn up into a curly ponytail. And suddenly, just like that, we're kissing— hard, fast, right there in the middle of the deserted special collections room. Trudy shoves me back against the glass case and sweeps my shirt over my head without bothering to unbutton it. Just as quickly, she unclasps my bra and bares my breasts, claiming them hotly with her mouth.

"What if someone..." I begin, between gasps, but Trudy bites my nipple, drawing a cry from me, and laughs throatily.

"I locked the door." She leans back to pluck a ring of keys from her dress pocket. "Perks of working the reference desk. Saw you coming up here and hoped you'd be in the mood for some companionship." Then she flings the keys to the floor and, gazing at me slyly, slides her hand into my pants. "You are in the mood— aren't you?"

"Oh, God..." I moan, throwing my head back as her fingers move between my panties and my stomach and then lower, seeking, *finding*— "Trudy..."

"Alex. I missed you." She kisses me, stealing my breath, even as her fingers continue to massage my aching core. "It upset me," she whispers against my mouth, her tongue flicking against my tongue, "how much I missed you. Wanted you. That isn't like me, you know." She pushes inside of me, moving her hand in a delicious rhythm, and she licks my throat, sucks on my breasts. White stars bloom and burst behind my closed eyes.

"But then I realized that it's okay for me to want you. It's okay for me to think about you...a *lot*. As long as you're thinking about me, too. So..."

I lift my lids to look at her, the sweet-sexiness of her, and she bites her lower lip, sliding her fingers upward to make soft circles over my clit.

"Have you been thinking about me, tiger?"

I whisper, "Every day," and reach out for her, pull her mouth to mine. I'm breathless, dizzy, near climax already, but Trudy slides her hand out of my pants and undoes the button, the zipper, sliding my khakis—along with my panties—over my legs and down to the floor. Then she smacks my bottom and points her chin toward the display case. "Up you go."

"What? On the *case*? We'll break it—"

"It can withstand a thousand pounds of pressure. I read the specs when I ordered it. Look." With expert fingers, Trudy unzips the front of her dress and steps out of it; she's naked, pink and perfect, underneath. Still wearing her black high heels, she boosts herself onto the glass cabinet effortlessly and then stands up on it, striking a pin-up girl pose. Her blonde hair glows beneath the soft, diffused lighting.

Grinning wickedly, she bends at the knees and

offers a hand to me. "I'm afraid I'll lose my balance if you don't join me up here. C'mon. Don't tell me you're scared of heights. You've climbed the pyramids in Egypt, haven't you? This oughta be a piece of cake."

Laughing softly, I kick off my shoes, boost myself onto the case and stand in front of Trudy, our nipples grazing. Her hand seeks out my wetness, and my hand, too, searches hers. As we entwine, our mouths crash together in a kiss that leaves me panting and aching. And feeling a little out of sorts. I've never been so drawn to a woman... Everything about her— her voice, her playful teasing, her hot bared skin, her cupcakes-and-paper scent—pulls me in like a moth to the light. Honestly, Trudy isn't even my type, or what I imagined my type to be. *Lucia's* my type: tall, dark and smoldering; earthy but cool; forward but private; physically available but emotionally removed...

Still, when I lie down in my bed every night, I'm not fantasizing about Lucia. The moment I close my eyes, I see Trudy's smile, remember our night together on the dusty floor, and feel piercingly alone. Lonely for her.

It's weird. New and weird, like everything is turning out to be in Niagara Falls. But, as Trudy said, maybe this kind of weird is okay. Maybe we should indulge our attraction to each other right now, see where this—whatever *this* is—leads us...

And maybe I should ask her for her phone number, for God's sake.

I'm not certain how we end up lying down, but suddenly I'm arching on top of Trudy, pressing her into the cold glass, moving my fingers inside of her as my lips and teeth taste and bite her neck and her large, blushing breasts. Her hand is still exploring me; I throb around her in an increasingly urgent rhythm. And then it's too much—too much heat, too much longing, too much sensation—and I give in to the waves, feel the orgasm crest through me. At the same time, Trudy cries out, clutching my shoulder, spasming against my hand for a long, gasping moment.

"Oh, my God," she breathes a minute later, her cheek soft and warm against mine. "We came *together*. That's never happened to me before." Her mouth catches my mouth, kissing me lingeringly, deeply. "Another first. Know what, tiger?"

"What?"

"You're awesome," she smiles, then kisses me again, harder, spiking my already stampeding heart rate and making my toes curl.

I chuckle and draw back from her, rising onto my elbow to peer down at her face—still flushed, alight, her blue-violet eyes hooded and sleepy. She looks so calm. So present. So lovely.

"You're awesome, too," I whisper. "You're...astonishing." Mystified, I shake my head, lick my lips. "I didn't expect you, Trudy Strange."

"I do like to surprise people."

I trail my fingertips over her inner arm, causing her to flutter her dark lashes. Then I grin. "I hate surprises. But you're my favorite kind of surprise. The good kind. Like the trowel my father gave me for my fourth birthday."

"You're comparing me to a *trowel?*" Her mouth slants, amused.

"Hey, it was my *first* trowel. It meant I was growing up. It meant I could dig in the dirt, just like my dad, and hunt for treasure."

"You're lucky, you know." She glides a cool

finger over my lips. "To be so passionate about your career. To seek out adventures—and get paid for it." Her chest rises and falls in a small sigh. For a moment, she's silent, thinking. Then she breathes, "That's what I want."

I blink at her. "You do?"

"Yeah." She lowers her eyes, suddenly shy. "You'll think it's silly. I mean...being a reference librarian is a *little* like digging for treasure. But it isn't adventurous so much as monotonous. Sometimes the copy machine breaks. And that's as exciting as it gets around here."

I tilt my head, curious. "Well, how would you rather spend your time?"

She peers up at me and blushes adorably, resting a hand against the side of my neck. "Okay. The thing is, I get such a *rush* when I'm ghost-hunting. Oh, my God, it's like nothing else. Well, it isn't better than *sex*." Her knee moves coyly between my legs. "But it's close enough." She holds up a finger. "Hey, don't forget your promise about my pink jumpsuit. I'm going to hold you to it."

"Please do," I smile, kissing her, warmth rushing through me as I imagine undressing her at some future point in time. Even after our exhaustive lovemaking this afternoon, and after that life-changing simultaneous orgasm, I'm still aching for her. I still want more...

But I came to the library today to ask Trudy a specific question, and, in my, well, *distraction*, I haven't gotten around to it yet. So I clear my throat, smile sheepishly. "I was wondering... Trudy, can I hire you?"

"Hire me? Oh, you mean, to research those Victorian archaeologists—"

"No, no. I mean"—I kiss her lightly—"to go all Scooby Doo in my house."

Her eyes widen. "You want me to bust your ghost?"

"I...guess?" I laugh. "Well, I don't want her busted, exactly. My sister and nephew are staying with me right now, to help me renovate the house, and we're all a little creeped out by the haunted happenings. Yesterday we saw a *second* ghost."

"No way!"

"Yes way. Another female ghost. And I think..." I shift my gaze to the case beneath us, my eyes resting on the drawing of Victoria to our immediate left. Victoria, Elizabeth's model. Victoria the ghost. A chill runs through me as I stare into the portrait's eyes and remember the *ghost's* eyes—hardly there, only gaps in the fog. I tap on the glass over the drawing. "I think that ghost was her. Victoria. And the other—the one we saw together—is the artist, Elizabeth."

Trudy peers down at the drawing, and then she stares at me, speechless.

"So...what do you say? You can bring your whole team. We just want to know what's going on, why their spirits are unsettled... How they're connected to each other, if they are. Do you think you'd be available to—"

"Yes. Yes! I mean, I'll have to clear it with everyone on the team, but how does tomorrow night sound? Around seven?"

I laugh again, charmed by her enthusiasm. "Sounds perfect." I press my mouth to her breast, and then I lift my gaze to meet her dark, smoky eyes. "I'll look forward to seeing you. I...feel different when I'm with you. Like..." I frown, considering.

"Like what?"

I sigh, look down at Trudy, and graze my thumb in semicircles over her forehead. "You make me feel like someone else. Someone I didn't know I had inside of me."

"Does that scare you?" she whispers, watching me.

"Yeah." I chuckle softly. "It scares me more than the ghosts, to be honest."

She nods, her lips curving into a small, weak smile. "Me, too. I can't stop thinking about you. When my FWB—friend with benefits—Ruby called me yesterday for a hook-up, I turned her down. Like, right away."

Now I smooth my thumb over Trudy's delicately arched brow. "Why?" I ask her, leaning down to kiss her shoulder.

She rakes a hand through my messy brown curls. "Because I only wanted you."

I take her breast in my mouth again, teasing her nipple with my tongue, as my fingers trail lightly over her skin. We kiss, kiss madly, smearing the glass beneath us as we move together...

And then the loudspeaker announces: *Trudy, patron waiting for you at the Reference Desk.*

"Damn it," Trudy laughs reluctantly, her breath hot against my ear, the heel of her hand pressed against my wetness. "Duty calls. I was on break, but my break is *definitely* over. We have been up here for...a while."

With feline grace, she disentangles her limbs from mine and lowers her high-heeled feet to the floor. Then, in one easy motion, she steps into her dress and zips it up, her eyes never leaving mine, her lips pink, swollen from my kisses. "How do I look?" She smooths down her rumpled ponytail. "Like I just got ravished?"

Still lying on my side on the case, I smile up at her. "Kinda."

"Good." Trudy leans over me and pinches my nipple as she gifts me with the French kiss to end all French kisses. Hell, to *redefine* the French kiss. "I'll be thinking about you as I, well, reference things. See you tomorrow night. With my pink jumpsuit on."

"Can't wait."

And with that, Trudy blows me a kiss and walks away, leaving me—alone and glaringly naked—in the special collections room. I dress quickly, my muscles deliciously sore, and soon follow in Trudy's footsteps. When I walk past her desk, she's chatting animatedly with a gray-haired woman in a tweed suit, but she pauses to wink at me as I lift my hand, my fingers still sweet with her scent, and wave good-bye.

❧❦❧

When I get home from the library, I sprawl on my bed and distract my brain from rampant, raunchy thoughts of Trudy by reading for the rest of the evening. I don't learn much of interest about Elizabeth, aside from the fact that she never married and died young, suddenly, from an undiagnosed illness that she contracted, her doctors assumed, during her travels.

Her father was abroad in England when his valet Xavier found Bess lying on her bedroom floor—*my* bedroom floor now—and assumed, at first, that she had fainted. But Bess wasn't breathing, though her bright green eyes were still open, still shining, according to the valet, "like a pair of glass marbles."

Elizabeth's father's health went into immediate decline, and he died a few months afterward, presumably of a broken heart. His layabout brother Thomas inherited his assets, including this house—which he willfully neglected, allowing it to fall into disrepair.

Patton Papers lived on, though, and lives on to this day, providing the world with greeting cards and stationery for every occasion. My mother used to buy packs of blank Patton cards printed with the image of a brown rabbit, her favorite animal; she sent correspondence on them to her friends in Canada whenever we were abroad.

Sighing, I shut the library book and roll over onto my back, staring up at the water-damaged ceiling. This house was once so full of love, *bursting* with love—until the tragedy of Elizabeth's death befell it. Is that why her spirit can't find rest? Because she's still mourning what she had, what she can never have again?

*Never* again, no matter how hard she wishes for it?

Just like I'll never see my father, my mother again—

Tears sting my eyes.

God...

I press the palms of my hands against my eyelids, as if to push the tears away. But they come; they always come when my thoughts turn to my parents, and my parents' accident. Years have passed, so many years, but the weight of their loss still hits me when I'm least expecting it, hits me so hard in the chest that it steals my breath, knocks the wind right out of me.

My sister and I used to sneak out of our house at night to go to this ruined playground a couple of blocks away: broken slides, see-saws split down the middle. But there was one intact swing, the kind suspended on chains with a narrow rubber seat. So we'd take turns on the swing, pushing one another recklessly high, pointing our toes toward the dim scattering of stars.

And then, when the swing got as high as it could go, we dared each other to jump off into the air. Cordelia—always more agile and athletic than me— landed on her feet, like a cat. Every time I jumped, though, I smacked the dusty ground so hard that all of the oxygen was pushed out of my lungs. For seconds, I couldn't breathe, could only lie there, gasping. I didn't want my big sister to think I was a weakling, so I never turned down her dares. But my blood pressure rises even now, reliving the sensation of sailing out against the sky, dreading the inevitable *thwack* against the earth.

The day that my parents died, I felt, again, like that little girl who leapt: unable to breathe, unable to move, unable to *be*. Helpless. Adrift.

Throughout the funeral, I kept picturing myself jumping off of the swing and falling, falling, falling, never knowing when the impact would come, never knowing when the pain would climax, or ease, or end.

It still hasn't ended.

Because I feel that way all over again in moments like these, when I remember how my father's stubbly chin felt beneath my fingertips. When I remember the way that my good-humored mother used to say *treasure* in a faux French accent: *tres-zure!* When I remember how much life they both had in them, how much life was burned up, senselessly, that day...

I fist the tears from my eyes and sit on the edge of the bed, resting my hands on my knees.

*Calm down, Alex.*

I'll never get over losing them. Maybe I'm not supposed to.

I can only hope that they, unlike Elizabeth, unlike Victoria, are at peace—and together. They have to be together.

Please let them be together...

I pause, and my eyes widen then, wondering.

Is *that* what Elizabeth and Victoria want? To be together?

My phone startles me from my thoughts, ringing on top of the suitcase that I've been using as a bedside table. I glance at the screen, register the number with some surprise.

Lucia.

Lucia? Why would *she* be calling me?

I temple my hands beneath my chin for a moment, considering whether or not to answer. I'm not feeling up to a conversation. But maybe this is important. She's probably calling from Cairo, after all...

"Lu?" I croak into the receiver, then clear my throat. "Hey. What's up?"

"Oh, it's... Wow. It's *you*. Your voice, Alex. Did I ever tell you that you have the sexiest voice? If I didn't, I'm telling you now. You have the *sexiest* voice."

Despite the tears pooled at the corners of my eyes, I laugh softly, shaking my head even as I wipe my damp cheeks with the back of my hand. "Don't tell me you called just to hear my voice. I know you aren't that sentimental, Lu."

"No, no. I—well, I have a proposition for you."

"Uh-oh. The last time you said that, you tied me to the tent poles..."

"Mm, that's right." She chuckles, her voice velvety smooth. Lucia is Italian, born in Venice to a gondolier, and her melodic accent never fails to thrill me. My heart skips a beat; I lick my lips, sinking back against my pillow.

"If I recall correctly," she says, "you quite *enjoyed* being tied to the tent poles, Alex."

A blush creeps over my chest, my face, as I switch the phone to my other ear and stand up, walking over to the vanity mirror. I'm red all over, and my sore eyes are saucer-wide. Somehow, it feels wrong to flirt with Lucia, if only over the telephone, when—

When what?

Trudy and I aren't exclusive. We haven't even exchanged phone numbers. I don't know where she lives, how she lives. I don't know her background, her belief system, her political views, whether she's a cat person or a dog person, her favorite ice cream flavor.

Still...

"So, what's the proposition?" I prompt Lucia matter-of-factly, raking a hand back through my messy curls with a shaky sigh.

"Ah, all business, are we?" I wince, detecting the disappointment in Lucia's tone. But she pauses for only a moment before saying, in her natural, nonchalant way, "Well, okay. Here's the thing. I've been contracted by that team in Mexico City, like I told you, and since I've got to book a connecting flight, anyway, I wondered if you'd mind a visit before I head out to the excavation site. Say, in two weeks? I could fly in to Buffalo, see your house, see *you*..." She trails off suggestively. "You know, for old times' sake."

"Old times? We haven't been apart that long, Lucia," I laugh softly, nervously, though my pulse is pounding.

"It's a figure of speech. What, are you stalling?" Lucia is nothing if not observant. That's what makes her great at her job—and amazing in bed. I glance over at my bed now and imagine Lucia there; my heartbeat quickens even as my stomach twists uneasily. "If you don't want me to come, Alex, just say so. We're both adults, yes? There's no sense in playing games with one another. I only thought—"

"Sorry, sorry. Of course I want to see you, Lu." The words taste bitter in my mouth, and I grimace at my reflection, inwardly cursing. *What am I saying?* Then again... My brain makes some hasty calculations. Two weeks from now, Cordelia and Jack will be back home in Toronto. And maybe Trudy will have tired of me, grown bored of my face, of my ghosts...

The thought makes my heart contract in my chest.

I draw in a deep breath, take a moment to reorient my thoughts—and summon some courage. "It's just..."

"Oh, God. What's wrong?"

"Okay." I force out a laugh, lower my voice. "I should warn you. You might be disappointed by my place. It has all the modern conveniences now—electricity, plumbing. It's practically a hotel."

"Well, we could always camp out in the backyard, right? Share a tent?"

"Mm." I swallow.

"Besides, I won't mind some pampering before the dig. It's an all-male crew, aside from me."

"Ugh."

"I know. Imagine the state of those toilets. Anyway," she purrs, voice honeyed, husky, "What do you say? I'm looking forward a rendezvous."

I sit back down on my mattress, folding my legs beneath me, eyes lingering on a portrait of Victoria Richards and the roughly sketched waterfall crashing behind her back. I wonder, abstractly, whether Elizabeth or Victoria is in the room with me now, invisible and listening to my conversation. If I were a ghost, I would take full advantage of every eavesdropping opportunity, but those proper Victorian ladies may have shinier morals than I do.

Suddenly, a flicker of light winks in my peripheral vision. I glance toward the vanity, and an orb, like the one I saw on my first night in the house, streaks out of the mirror and shoots through the window.

I'm too startled to react, and Lucia is still speaking: "...you know, I haven't seen the falls, so I'm counting on you to show me...all of the sights."

Heart beating fast, I force myself to ignore the orb, to focus, instead, on the conversation. I *need* to stay focused, because when Lucia says *all of the sights,* I know full well that she isn't referring to Niagara Falls—or any of its associated tourist traps. Her tone, as always, drips with sex—the taste of it, the scent of it; I feel undressed, *licked* by her voice alone. A shiver courses through my body—along with the remnants of fear—as I bite my lower lip and exhale a shaky breath.

Then I say, all in a rush, "I've met someone."

"You—what?" She laughs curtly. "You *met* someone. Well, what do you mean? A female someone?"

"Mm-hmm."

"I see..." Lucia pauses, considering. "Hey, I'm up for it. The more the merrier."

"No." My face flushes. "No, no, I mean... I'm sorry, Lu. This is... This is different. I think."

"Different," she repeats, her tone dull, flat. "Different from me, you mean."

"Different from...from everyone." As the words leave my mouth, I feel the truth of them reverberate. Trudy *is* different. She's different than anyone, everyone, I've ever known. And *I* feel different when I'm with her.

I feel *better.*

"Have to admit, Alex, you've caught me off guard. I never suspected that you, of all people—"

"Me, neither."

"Well, congratulations. I guess." She exhales a heavy sigh. "You're a fast one, aren't you? Oh, I'm being awful. No, really, I'm happy for you. I'm unhappy for *me.* Thought we'd have one last lusty week together... God, you're a great kisser. Did I ever tell you that? When you kiss me, I feel it all the way down to my—"

"Lu—"

"Right. Well, *ciao.* I promised to help Giorgio clean up the common area; it's littered with beetle shells. Another infestation. Gross. But pretty. Um... Keep in touch? No, that's stupid. We won't keep in touch. Have a nice life. And, really, I *am* happy for you."

"Thanks. *Ciao,* Lu." After I hang up, I cradle my cell phone in my hand for several minutes, staring at the dark screen, listening to the blood pound in my ears, my eyes restlessly darting between the mirror and the window. I should have been excited about a visit from Lucia. I should have started making plans, gathering, *ahem*, accoutrements for our nights together...

But, instead, I just felt a cold kind of dread. I didn't only feel as if I would be betraying Trudy.

I felt as if I'd be betraying myself.

I shake my head, simultaneously irritated and confused.

To work off my frustration and try to forget the phone call and the supernatural sighting in my room, I pass a couple of hours polishing the upstairs floors. The hardwood gleams like dark amber when I'm finished. Confusion sucks, but it's an excellent motivator. And all of that hard work tires me out. When I collapse into bed in the wee hours of the morning, tossing my library books to the floor, I fall asleep instantly, into looping dreams of Victoria— always reaching, whispering, her dress whipping around her ankles as the spray from the falls dampens her tear-stained face...

# Chapter Six

I frown at the small black box positioned in the middle of my entryway floor. It's square and unmarked, and it's emitting steady white noise, like radio static, so I can hardly hear what Trudy and her fellow Ghost Team members are murmuring to one another. The four of them stand gathered a few feet away from my sister and me, heads bowed together, foreheads wrinkled in concentration. When I strain my ears, I catch some words here and there: *EVP, poltergeist, residual haunting...*

A disbelieving smile forms on my lips as I consider how unlikely all of this is. I feel as if I've wandered onto a movie set—well, not the set of a horror movie, really, but of a horror movie *spoof*, because, in those hot pink jumpsuits, it's kind of hard to take the Ghost Team seriously. They look like a tribute to the '80s: all they need is poofier hair and some glam rock makeup to complete the look.

Trudy, though...

Hot pink is unquestionably her color.

And though she's engaged in earnest conversation with her fellow teammates, she sneaks conspiratorial glances at me: a smirk, a wink, an appreciative appraisal. And her fingers keep toying with the zipper of her jumpsuit, tugging it down and then back up, exposing more cleavage than is publicly appropriate—before sealing the creamy pink skin away again.

I lick my lips and distract myself with thoughts of ice cubes, icebergs, ice cream headaches...while, by my side, Cordelia casts me a knowing look and mouths, *Nice friend*.

"So, Alex," begins the man Trudy introduced as Igor. He *looks* like an Igor, frankly, with bushy black brows and a drooping mouth, as if he's in a constant state of disapproval. He's the loudest of the ghost-hunting group, the most intimidating, unapologetically unfriendly. When we first met ten minutes ago, he refused to shake my hand. Maybe it's a germ phobia thing, but I got the feeling that he just doesn't like me. And, if so, the feeling is mutual.

"Describe the manifestations you've experienced," he says in a bored, authoritative tone. "And use the four-S guideline: sight, smell, sound, sensation."

The dark-haired, middle-aged woman standing to Igor's right—Marisol—places a hand on his shoulder; he shrugs it off and steps away from her, scowling. "Oh, Igor." Marisol smiles indulgently, almost fondly, at him. Then she bends down to turn off the static-emitting box and focuses her attention on me. "What Igor means, Ms. Dark, is we'd like an account of how the ghosts looked, whether there was any change in temperature during their appearances, and if they spoke to you, made any sounds at all. We've heard Trudy's account of the staircase ghost already. Now we'd like to hear your side of things."

"Oh, okay." I glance at Trudy uncertainly. She offers me a warm smile and a nod of her blonde head, encouraging me to speak. I clear my throat, summoning up the memory of the two apparitions.

"Well, the ghosts were like mist...kind of...and light," I begin haltingly. "But they had shape. They were definitely, um, woman-shaped." I meet Trudy's gaze, and her lips curve up into a flirtatious smile. She's wearing shiny pink lip gloss and a sparkly pink eyeshadow that emphasizes her blue-violet eyes.

"Go on," Igor mutters, impatient.

"Right." I bite my lip, shake my head. "I recognized one of the ghosts," I say, looking up toward the stained glass window and indicating it with my chin. "Elizabeth Patton. Former resident. She looked the same as she does in that window up there—same age, same hairstyle, long dress. Only she was less colorful and more..." I smile weakly. "Ghost-like, I guess. Floating right above the stairs."

"And the other sighting?" This prompt comes from Ruby—*Ruby*, as in, Trudy's friend-with-benefits Ruby.

Granted, Trudy might know more than one woman named Ruby, but the Ruby standing before me is undoubtedly queer. Aside from her gaydar-activating aura, the *Dip me in honey and throw me to the lesbians* button pinned to her jumpsuit kind of clued me in. Her bleached white hair is short, almost a buzz cut, and her eyes are shockingly green—too green, lime green. Contacts, maybe. She has a long, lean, lanky silhouette, similar to—I'm chagrined to note—my body type.

Yeah. So Trudy has a type.

I thought I had a type, too...until I met her.

God, am I *jealous*?

Ruby's staring at me, her strange eyes narrowed, a frown downturning her lips, and she grips a little notepad in her hands, pencil poised, awaiting my response. Has Trudy told her about me? Does she know that Trudy and I—

"Alex?" Trudy watches me curiously, confused, I assume, by my silence. "Anything wrong? Do you want to take a break? We could—"

"No, sorry." I cross my arms, exhale a small sigh, and look to Marisol, avoiding Ruby's—and Trudy's—gazes. "The other sighting took place outside, in the backyard. I wasn't the only witness. My sister"—I nod to Cordelia—"and her son Jack were there, too. They saw the ghost before I did, actually."

"And where is Jack?" Ruby asks, trailing her green gaze along the steps, as if she suspects we've tucked him away upstairs.

And, in fact, we have. Jack is playing in the middle bedroom with the junior archaeologist kit that I bought him this morning from the Boulevard Mall. The box promised "hours of fun," so Cordelia and I are hoping that the indoor projects will keep him busy for as long as the Ghost Team is here. We discussed it, and neither of us feels comfortable with exposing him to paranormal questioning. We're still coming to terms with his I-see (and speak to)-dead-people revelations, after all.

"He won't be joining us tonight." I meet Ruby's probing gaze and hold it; after a long, tense moment, she glances away. "But I'd be happy to take you out to the backyard, and Cordelia and I can show you where the ghost appeared."

"Well," Trudy says quickly, gesturing to her cat-face wristwatch, "we've got to move things along. It's already seven-thirty, and Marisol has to be home with her kids by ten. Igor, Marisol, Ruby—why don't the three of you and Cordelia go out into the backyard? Record her experience, and I'll start setting up in here with Alex. Igor, install a camera on the exterior of the house. Marisol, run a couple of EVP sessions—"

"And what should I do, Trudy, while you're"—Ruby slides her gaze over me, her eyes narrowing almost imperceptibly—"setting up?" She over-enunciates the final two words, making it crystal-clear that by "setting up" she means...something else. Though she pastes on a small smile, it looks grotesque, unsettling, in contrast to her glowering gaze.

"Oh, the usual." Trudy regards Ruby with a calm, natural curve to her lips, tilting her blonde head to one side. "Use your Spidey senses, Rube. See if anyone tries to get in touch with you."

"While you get in *touch* in here. Right?"

Unflustered, Trudy ignores Ruby's insinuation and explains, for my and Cordelia's benefit, "Ruby's our team clairvoyant. She makes a living reading palms for the tourists. Unlike most of the mediums in Niagara Falls, though, Ruby's the real deal."

"Aw, shucks." Ruby pretends to be flattered, but her expression gradually shifts, darkens, and I notice, with a sinking feeling in my stomach, that her nails have been filed to sharp points. "Hey, maybe the sisters would like to have their palms read?" She directs the question to Cordelia and me, but her eyes are, uncomfortably, locked onto mine. "Free of charge."

Predictably, Cordelia's jaw drops. "Sure! Thanks! Oh, my God, I've always wanted to have my palm read. I went to a psychic fair once but chickened out at the last minute. How about you, Alex? You'll do it with me, won't you?"

I smile weakly, gazing through the window at the dim, littered street. "Think I'll pass."

"Shame." Ruby shakes her head, green eyes

flashing. I realize, all of the sudden, that Ruby reminds me a little of a girl I knew back in Canada. Tessie Langford. I pined after Tessie for months, and after we finally hooked up—with the understanding that we weren't dating exclusively—she started getting jealous of every woman breathing within ten feet of me.

So a week later, we ended our relationship. But every once in a while, Tessie sends me an overly friendly, creepily informed-about-my-life email, suggesting that we "grab a cup of coffee sometime." On a hunch, I Googled her name and found out that she'd been issued restraining orders by four different women.

In all likelihood, Ruby isn't a stalker, just a friend with benefits whose feelings have been hurt. If Ruby knows who I am, I can't blame her for being snappish with me. Trudy's awesome, and I've been monopolizing her lately. Well, I'm not sure that *monopolizing* is the right word for what I've done with her...

Ruby interrupts my thoughts, says, "There's no better way to get to know somebody than through their hands. But you know that, Alex. You and Tru have already gotten to know one another's hands pretty well. Haven't you?"

Okay. Trudy *definitely* told Ruby about me.

Through gritted teeth, Trudy hisses, "Ruby. Outside. Now." She takes the woman's arm and guides her to the back door, gesturing for everyone else to follow. They carry their bags of equipment outside, murmuring softly, and after a few moments, Trudy returns, wearing an apologetic expression.

"God, I didn't know Ruby would react like this. I shouldn't have told her who you are, but we have this honesty policy, and I didn't want her to figure it out for herself and then feel betrayed—God. I'm sorry, Alex. She's never been jealous before." She pauses in front of me, reaches out to clasp my hand. Her head is bowed so that her long lashes cast shadows onto her cheeks. She laughs softly and whispers, "Then again, she's never had *reason* to be jealous before."

I touch my fingers to her chin, and she raises her eyelids, gazing up at me with her breath-stealing, dusky gaze. I kiss her—gently. Then...not so gently. My hands slide around her waist, meeting at her back, and I draw her close, as close as two bodies can get...

When our mouths part, she rests her chin on my shoulder and breathes out a long, laughing sigh. "Alex... What are you doing to me?"

"Same thing you're doing to me, I think."

Chuckling again, Trudy claims my mouth, sliding her hands beneath my shirt, beneath my bra, cupping my breasts with her warm, smooth palms. "I know we're here to bust some ghosts, but I don't want to do anything but kiss you," she smiles against my lips.

"No arguments here..."

Just then, my phone begins to vibrate in my pants pocket.

Trudy laughs huskily. "Gonna answer that? Go on. I'll keep myself busy." She bows her head and nudges beneath my shirt, licking my stomach as she moves upward, her hands still massaging my nipples, then squeezing... "Answer, Alex," she grins against me.

I chuckle and slide the cell out of my pocket, glance at the screen—and then I drop the phone into my pocket again.

"Wrong number?"

"Um...no." I lick my lips. "Just someone from my past."

Trudy pauses as her mouth closes over my nipple. She pulls her head out of my shirt and straightens, regarding me seriously. "Someone from your past—as in...a woman?"

I shrug slightly and nod. "Yeah."

"Oh. Oh. Yeah. Cool. What's her name?" Trudy's trying to act casual, but her face fell when I confirmed her suspicion, and there's a little treble in her voice that wasn't there before.

"Trudy—"

"No, I'm just curious. I'm just...getting to know you. And your past is part of you. It's everything that came before this moment. We need to talk more, you know?"

"Yeah, we do." Sighing, I lift my gaze to the ceiling and murmur, "Lucia. Her name's Lucia."

"Ah. *Lucia.*" Trudy's fingers seek out my nipples again and pinch them—not too hard, just enough to send a lightning flash of longing throughout my body. I moan, leaning against her. "See? That was easy. Sharing. Just as easy as *Sesame Street* always promised it would be. And sharing has its own rewards..." One of her hands slips loose from my bra and glides down along my abdomen, slipping beneath the waistline of my pants, beneath my panties...

I moan again.

We fall against one another, kissing deeply, desperately—until Trudy trails her lips over my neck, lingering at my collarbone. "Problem is," she whispers, "we've got a job to do. And I'm team leader. What kind of example am I setting here? God, you taste so good," she murmurs, kissing me again. But then, "Oh, c'mon," she pouts. "Be my sexy assistant." And just like that, her warmth leaves me, and she's tugging on my hand, casting me a coy glance as she pulls me over to a pile of electronics. Ghost-hunting equipment.

Right. The ghosts. *That's* why we're here tonight.

Empty-armed, unkissed, I gaze up at Elizabeth Patton-in-the-window and offer her a beleaguered, but resigned, smile.

Okay. Once more with feeling: icebergs, ice cubes, ice cream headaches...

❧ ⟨◉⟩ ❧

Funny how quickly you can get the hang of something new when you're thrust into an unfamiliar situation. By nine-thirty, I feel like a ghost-hunting pro, taking slow, quiet steps through the house with my EVP recorder in hand. Trudy taught me the basics: ask questions aloud, move as soundlessly as possible, and take account of any noises, natural or supernatural. So far, I haven't experienced a single ghostly encounter, but EVPs—electronic voice phenomena—according to Igor, are not always audible to the naked ear. Sometimes paranormal voices are picked up by the recorder only, so after tonight's investigation, the team is going to listen to the audio footage, watch the video footage, and report back to me with their findings.

I'm not optimistic: all in all, it's been a disappointing, uneventful night.

Hard to tell with a grumpy guy like Igor, but based upon the frustrated looks he's been assailing me with, I think he's beginning to suspect that I made everything up, that this old Victorian isn't haunted.

After all, Ruby hasn't conversed with any lost souls, and Trudy's had no luck with her various and very complicated-looking electronic gadgets.

And we've only got half an hour left.

As of five minutes ago, the six of us split up, armed with voice recorders or video cameras. Trudy, Cordelia and I are inside of the house, and Ruby, Igor and Marisol are wandering around the exterior.

Right now, I'm sitting on my bed, feeling more than a little absurd as I talk to the empty air, asking Elizabeth and Victoria to "give me a sign" as I hold up my voice recorder and wait, listening hard for a spectral response.

Nothing. Not a whisper or a whine.

I have to admit, if I were a ghost, I'd bristle at being ordered to speak and perform on command. If I were a ghost, I'd hold my tongue until this investigation was over, playfully, stubbornly silent. Lurking, waiting, soundlessly laughing—

And, just then, someone *does* laugh.

"What the hell—"

I spring up from the mattress, wielding my voice recorder like a knife. *Relax, Alex.* Maybe the voice belonged to Trudy or Cordelia...though it didn't sound like either of them. It was a female voice but light, musical. Creepy. And right beside my ear.

I glance down at my arms, covered in goosebumps; a cool gust of air engulfs my body, just like it did the first time I entered this room, on my tour with Marie. Marisol mentioned something earlier about temperature change... Does this mean that a ghost is nearby?

I start to call out for Trudy but stop myself— or, rather, my tongue suddenly becomes a useless lump in my mouth—and my numb fingers drop the voice recorder to the floor.

*Oh, my God...*

The laughing hasn't stopped, and I can see my breath coming out in little puffs of fog, but these things hardly register in my mind; *nothing* else registers aside from the vision before me: Elizabeth the ghost. Full-length, down to her boots, which are faintly red in the dim light of the room. She looks misty but *real*, so much more real than before, and she's smiling, laughing—laughing at me.

Or...no. Teasing me. Her eyes are dark but kind. My own eyes skim over her features: black lashes, straight nose, full lips above a rounded chin. Her neck is long and lovely as a swan's, and she has a tall, lean silhouette, buttoned tightly into her black lace gown.

"Can you hear me?" I whisper. My heart thuds, and I feel dizzy, dazed. Is this real? Am I dreaming? Did I fall asleep—

*"Yes..."* Elizabeth says, and just as quickly, her expression grows grave. I glimpse the sorrow behind her laughter; staring into her eyes, I feel, in my deepest core, an immeasurable sense of loss. A loss that isn't mine but that I know intimately—bone-deep, soul-aching, irreversible, inescapable...

I double over from the weight of it, force out between gasps, "You lost someone close to you?"

*"Yes."* It pains her to speak; she winced when she forced out *yes* before, and she does so again.

She's fading.

The Ghost Team informed Cordelia and me earlier that a spirit requires a large amount of energy in order to manifest. One reason that ghost hunters use electronic equipment to record paranormal presences is because the spirits can use the electricity, the batteries in those devices, as a power source. Maybe appearing to me, laughing at me, depleted Elizabeth's energy store. Her outline is growing less distinct, more transparent...

"What do you want?" I ask her, stepping closer, until we're only a few inches apart. The air is thinner, colder here, and Elizabeth looks like a hazy hologram, an illusion of light, when, before, she almost resembled a living, breathing person. "How can I help you?"

She gazes at me sadly, shakes her head. Barely there wisps of brown hair fall out of her elaborate topknot, gliding down to her shoulders. And then she lifts her arm and, without a word, points to the window.

I watch her for a moment, uncertain, hesitant. "You want me to look out the window?" She doesn't answer, only points and stares toward the panes. So I walk over to the window, acutely aware of Elizabeth's cold, misty presence at my back, and when I peer through the glass, gazing down at the dark, weedy backyard, my heart seizes in my chest.

Victoria is staring up at me.

Victoria the ghost. Elizabeth's art model. Elizabeth's...friend?

And everyone—Trudy, Cordelia, Ruby, Igor, Marisol—stands in a circle around Victoria, alternatively gaping at her and then gaping up at me. Cordelia flaps her arms like a bird, calling out words that I can't hear...

I turn back around, fully expecting to see no one, nothing, in my bedroom behind me, but Elizabeth is still here, arm lowered now, eyes lowered, too. She's as filmy as plastic wrap, particles of her form drifting in tiny orb-like shapes up, up, to disappear into the ceiling.

"Wait! What—I mean, how—who is Victoria to you? Are you looking for her? She's right out there. Come, look," I urge her, but she doesn't move, only continues to dissipate, to come apart. "Bess, please."

Her mouth curves softly at the sound of her nickname.

"Bess," I say again.

But it's too late; she's gone.

Still gaping, I fall onto my bed in a boneless heap, my heart hammering in an erratic rhythm. Gradually, the air grows warmer, and my goosebumps fade. But I can't stop staring at the space in the room that Elizabeth—Bess—had filled, as palpable and real as Trudy, as Cordelia.

And I can't erase the memory of the heartache she shared with me, the abysmal sense of loss that she communicated—for Victoria.

❧✦❧

"So." Marisol's brown eyes are as wide as the saucer resting beneath her teacup.

"So," Trudy echoes her, smiling broadly, brilliantly. She takes a triumphant swig of her coffee, squinting her eyes when the liquid burns her tongue. Unbothered, she shakes her blonde head, laughs, exclaims, "That was *epic*. Told you guys you wouldn't be disappointed. Full-body apparition! And Alex had a *conversation* with Elizabeth Patton! Whew. Okay, *now* what?"

I sip at my own coffee, faintly shaking my head. Marisol, Trudy, Igor, Ruby and I are sitting at a small table in Bean Power—conveniently open twenty-four hours, seven days a week—and we all look like, well, we just saw a ghost.

Or two ghosts, in my case.

Based upon our blanched, haunted expressions, the empathetic barista prescribed extra espresso and put on a "Soothing Vibes" CD. But the Enya song that's playing right now reminds me of Elizabeth's lilting voice, high, feminine, and eerie.

Poor Marisol's hand won't stop shaking enough to allow her to drink her tea.

"*Now*," Igor begins, crossing his arms over his large chest and exhaling loudly through his nose, "we examine the data, write up our individual reports, compare, contrast, compile—"

"Yeah, yeah, yeah." Ruby rolls her green eyes, leaning back in her chair until the front legs lift off of the floor. "We'll do all of that, Egon—"

"I*gor*—"

"—but what we need to do right *now* is get royally *wasted*. What do you say, Tru? Wanna blow this caffeine stand and hit the old Pink Lady?" She smiles at Trudy across the table, bedroom-eyed, tracing her tongue over her lips. "They've got a five-dollar cover tonight. And remember? Manic Pixie Nightmare Girls are playing. I bought us tickets last month. You *love* MPNG."

"Yeah. I do. But..." Trudy downs the rest of her coffee, wincing—and now I can't tell if she's wincing because the hot beverage burned her throat or because Ruby's invitation made her feel uneasy.

Gambling on the latter, I place a hand on her arm and smile nonchalantly. "Hey, it's been a crazy night. If you want to unwind at the club, go for it." *Go for it?* I don't even *talk* like that. And though I heard myself say the words, I can hardly believe that they came out of my mouth. I feel a little like a ventriloquist's dummy—or just a human dummy.

God, why did I *say* that?

"I should go?" Trudy asks, regarding me with surprise. "Oh. I thought we were going to, um, hang out later." Meaningfully, she toys with the zipper on her jumpsuit and raises a brow, her lip-glossed mouth drawn into a confused frown. "You changed your mind?"

I swallow and then dig myself a deeper grave: "No, I'm just tired. You know."

"Right. Yeah. I know. Yeah, it's been an adventure." She smiles weakly, avoiding my gaze.

Marisol stands up, slinging her purse over her shoulder. "Let's all catch up tomorrow, compare our findings, like Igor said. I've got to get home. I'm already twenty minutes late, and my sister will be leaving for her night shift soon. It was nice to meet you, Alex."

"You, too, Marisol. Thanks for your help."

Moments after Marisol leaves, Igor rises from the table, mutters something about the eleven-o'clock news, and makes an awkward, hasty exit.

"And then there were three," Ruby announces ominously, suctioning the last of her iced coffee through her straw. "Be right back." She stands up to toss her cup in the recycling bin before heading toward the unisex restroom at the back of the cafe.

"Alex—"

"Trudy—"

We laugh, having spoken in unison; I reach for Trudy's hands and enclose them with my own. Her fingers are cold, ice cold, so I hold them tighter.

"Look, it's not that I *want* you to go out with Ruby. Honestly, I really, *really* don't want you to—"

"You don't?"

"*God,* no." I smile, my gaze moving from her eyes to her mouth; her lips are slightly parted, shiny, temptingly pink... "I just...I don't know how to act around you. So I'm trying to be chivalrous. Self-sacrificing. To the point of stupidity. I'm lost. I've never done...this...before."

She smiles softly and lifts a brow. "This?"

"Yeah, *this*. Us. *You*."

"Ah." Her mouth slides into a smirk, and she slips one hand free to trail her long nails over my cheek, my neck... "Beg to differ there, tiger. You *have* done me before. Shall I jog your memory? There was that time on the floor—"

"I remember every moment." I bring the hand I'm still holding to my lips. "Every breath."

"A scientist *and* a romantic. You undersold yourself, Alex." She copies my gesture, drawing my hand to her hot mouth, kissing my fingers lingeringly, one by one. "So what do we do about all of these feelings of ours, Dr. Dark?"

I flick my gaze toward the swinging restroom door. Ruby just emerged and is aiming for our table, hands shoved deep into her jumpsuit pockets. Knowing that our time together is running out, I meet Trudy's searching gaze and whisper, "How about we just trust each other?"

"Trust. Huh. Yeah. Sure. I can do that. But really?" She indicates her jumpsuit, Vanna White-style. "You promised, Alex."

"And I always keep my promises. Another night. Or...day. Or, hell, *weekend*. Anyway, you shouldn't miss that concert."

"C'mon, Tru." Ruby reaches Trudy's side and points to the tie-dyed clock on the wall. "Show starts in fifteen minutes. Said on Facebook that they're gonna do some of their old stuff from the first album. Remixes, I think."

"Cool." Dragging her eyes from mine, Trudy stands up, yawns, stretches cutely, and then offers me a coy smile. "Stop by the library tomorrow, Alex, and I'll share my data with you. Pretty sure I'm in possession of some pretty wild stuff."

My mouth curves involuntarily. "I know you are."

Ruby groans.

Undaunted, Trudy picks up her half-full coffee cup and blows me a kiss. As she turns slightly, aiming for the door, Ruby snakes her arm through the loop of Trudy's elbow, guiding her out of Bean Power as she leans toward her, whispering something, her slanted lips grazing Trudy's ear...

"I'm an idiot," I moan quietly, and I cradle my head in my hands, trying *not* to envision the adrenaline-fueled night Trudy and Ruby are about to share—and, of course, failing miserably. They'll be hip to hip at the club, dancing, sweaty, a little or a lot drunk, and then Ruby will reach for Trudy's waist, draw her close as the music pumps hard around them—

No. *Stop.*

We swore to trust one another.

Granted...we didn't set any specific parameters for that "trust."

We didn't express, in so many words, that our newly minted trust meant neither of us would sleep with another woman...

But I think that was kind of implied.

Wasn't it?

I tug at my curls in frustration.

And to punish myself for being lackadaisical, too cool, too terrified to really *feel* a complex emotion, I down the rest of my mud-puddly coffee in one gulp, scalding my tongue and scarring my throat.

Ouch.

Okay, that should probably be my last cup of Desert Siesta for a while.

# Chapter Seven

Trudy picks up a palm-sized snow globe and shakes it, tossing glitter over a miniature scene of Niagara Falls. "They got it all wrong," she says, holding the globe up to her purple-lined eye and peering through the blue-tinted water. "Backwards. The Bridal Veil Falls are on the wrong side. See?"

I take the snow globe from her and gaze at the sparkly scene. The resin backdrop is sloppily painted in shades of sky blue and white, but there's a well-meaning charm about the tiny Victorian pair of women standing on a ledge in the foreground, wearing form-fitting black gowns and holding parasols. Shoulders brushing, they, like me, look toward the distant—albeit incorrectly positioned—cascades.

I flip the trinket over and glance at the price: five ninety-five. "I think I'm going to buy this," I say then, surprising myself.

"Really?" Trudy laughs, blue-violet eyes aglow beneath the fluorescent lights.

God, she's beautiful.

Today she's wearing her blonde hair loose, and her curves are sheathed in a vintage-style off-white dress printed with a pattern of Halloween cats—though Halloween is still weeks away. "Never too early to get your witch on," Trudy had winked at me when I first admired her ensemble at the library.

After she clocked out for her lunch break, we bought some veggie dogs from a food truck, and for the last twenty minutes or so, we've been wandering the streets, popping into the tacky shops selling Niagara Falls keychains and t-shirts and velvet paintings. And snow globes.

"My mom had this thing about snow globes," I explain, then cough into my hand. The air in here is warm—no, hot. Suffocating. I tug at the collar of my button-down shirt and shake my head, blinking. "She collected them. Bought one from every place she traveled. And because we came to Niagara Falls so often, she had about ten snow globes from here, all of them different. Some were actually kind of beautiful." I look through the glass globe in my hand, smiling faintly, remembering.

"She had one like this, with two women in it... When she showed it to me—I was eleven—something happened, changed, inside of me. Suddenly I felt brave enough to come out to her. And her reaction was...amazing. She acted like I'd just told her the grass was green, like it was the most natural, obvious thing. Like it was no big deal at all."

"That *is* amazing."

"Yeah." I hand the snow globe to the cashier, along with a ten-dollar bill.

"But...you said *had.*"

"What?" I accept my change and my bag and aim for the door, Trudy close by my side.

"Alex." In a softer voice, she repeats, "You said *had.* Your mom *had* a thing about snow globes. Does that mean—"

"Oh. Yeah." We step into the sunshine, and I tilt my head back to take in the white scatter of clouds overhead. When I meet Trudy's gaze, she's watching me with concern, with foreboding. I know that look... Instantly, I flash back to the funeral, to the glum, apologetic expressions that came over my parents' friends' faces when they met my eyes.

I shudder slightly but offer her a watery smile. "She died. My mom and my dad—there was an airplane crash over Peru and..." Glancing away, I sigh. "Ten years ago."

"Oh, my God. Alex..." Trudy slips her arm around my waist, squeezes gently. "I don't know what to say. That's awful."

"It was. It is." We walk toward the intersection; ahead, the multicolored lights of the sky-scraping casino flash garishly, offensively. I squint at them, shrugging. "Funny thing about grief—it doesn't really ever end. It's been years, but the hurt's always there, just beneath the surface. I guess it gets easier to push it down. But sometimes it shoots up like...like a geyser. You relive that pain all over again. No matter how much time passes, it never really goes away."

Self-conscious, I glance at Trudy and chuckle beneath my breath. "Sorry. I'm...in a weird mood. All of this ghost stuff... But you don't want to hear about—"

"No, I do. Alex, listen." We pause in front of an Indian restaurant; Trudy faces me, taking both of my hands, exhaling a deep breath. "I want to know you. I want to hear everything about you. We..." She laughs. "We're kind of like that snow globe. Backwards. We started backwards. Sex first—and we missed out on the getting-to-know-you bits."

"Hey, I've gotten to know your bits—"

"Set you up for that one." She winks coyly,

trailing a nail over the line of my cheek. "But I'm serious. Don't *edit* yourself around me. We both have a bad habit of keeping other people at arm's length—figuratively speaking, of course. Look..." Trudy drops my hands to rake her fingers through her blonde waves; a frown plays over her mouth, and her brows are furrowed. "I lost someone, too."

"You did?" I place a hand on her shoulder, drawing her close.

"My brother Truman. Twin brother. We weren't identical, obviously, and we didn't have a psychic bond or anything—I wish we *had*—but he was my brother. We went through everything together. That horrible private school. Our parents' divorce. Truman's divorce. My many—*many*—failed career adventures...and relationships. He was my best friend. We survived. Together." Her lower lip trembles. "Until we didn't. He got cancer and... God, it happened so fast—"

I pull her into my arms, whispering, "You were lucky to have each other. He was lucky to have *you*."

"Thanks." She leans back, wipes a tear from the corner of her eye. "It's been three years, but I still have his number programmed into my phone. Pathetic, right? But I can't bear to erase it. Sometimes I almost think I *smell* him nearby. Isn't that weird? He was always eating cucumbers," she laughs. "Sometimes it feels like he just went on vacation, or stepped out for a cigarette. I trick myself into believing that, anyway—whenever thinking about him hurts too much."

Eyes shining, Trudy twines her fingers with mine and tugs me along, further down the sidewalk, closer to the park bordering the falls. "Truman and I worked summers at the Cave of the Winds, just under the Bridal Veil Falls.  Handing out ponchos and slippers to tourists, telling them to watch their step as they walked over the stone staircase leading down to the cave."

"I love the Cave of the Winds."  I laugh softly. "I met my first post-coming out crush there, this girl with two ponytails named DeeDee."

"DeeDee?"

"Well, it was the eighties.  And I was—I don't know—fourteen?  Anyway, I wandered off from the tour group, and then I heard someone saying, *Hey! Hey!* And when I looked toward the waterfall, there she was. Cute and blonde, with a hundred-watt smile.  I couldn't help but follow her.  She snuck me back into the restricted area, said, *Hi, I'm DeeDee*, and then she kissed me.  A *lot*."  I smile.  "Until Cordelia caught us and dragged me away.  It's one of my best memories..."  I trail off, because I've realized that Trudy has stopped walking.  I search her eyes, am about to ask her why she's paused, but she's staring at me with the oddest expression: odd...but familiar—a mixture of awe and fear, as if she's seen a ghost.

I glance over my shoulder to make certain that Elizabeth and Victoria aren't floating somewhere behind me, but all I see is a family of living people wearing blue Maid of the Mist ponchos and eating bags of caramel popcorn.

"Alex, that—" Trudy breathes out, shakes her head, laughs—a small, tight-sounding laugh—before she swallows and confronts my gaze with wide, shining eyes.  "That was me."

"What?  What was you?"  I narrow my brows, confused.

"That girl.  That *kiss*.  Well, kiss*es*."

"Huh?" I tilt my head. "I don't—what are you talking about?"

In a half-frustrated, half-jubilant tone, Trudy says, "*I* was DeeDee," one hand pressed to her chest, her glittery orange nails poking into the fabric of her dress. "It was my childhood nickname. Trudy. DeeDee. When I started eleventh grade, I insisted that everyone call me Trudy or Tru, because I thought DeeDee made me sound young and naive." She bites her lip and regards me with her delicate brows raised. "I was never naive."

"Whoa." I turn around, walk a few steps in the opposite direction, nearly colliding with the poncho-clad family; kernels of popcorn drop to the sidewalk as they step aside. I turn around again, crunching popcorn beneath my heels and dragging my hand through my hair. "Wait. You were—you're serious? You aren't kidding? That was really *you?*"

"It was really me." Trudy smiles faintly, though her skin has paled. She looks bewildered, shaken. "I was fourteen, too. And I thought about you. I knew you were a tourist—only tourists do the touristy things—so I figured my chances of ever seeing you again were next to nothing. Zero. But I still wished for it. Dreamed of you. Alex..." Trudy curves her fingers through my belt loops and draws me close, chest to chest, hip to hip. "You were my first real kiss."

I blink at her, speechless.

And then our mouths collide—hot, wet, urgent—right there in the center of the sidewalk. A minute, two minutes later, we part, gasping, and lean our foreheads together, lips still parted, grazing. "This is all so..." I begin, searching for the right word.

"I know." Trudy laughs huskily and offers me

a cunning smile. Despite eating that veggie dog, her breath smells like cake, like candy. "Remember that book I showed you the first time we met in the library?"

"Mm-hmm." I smirk. "The New Agey one with the clouds and rainbows on the cover—"

*"Everything Happens for a Reason."*

"Yeah." My smirk fades, replaced by an uncertain frown.

But what are the chances of my meeting and falling for the girl who kissed me in the Cave of the Winds two decades ago? About the same odds as my buying a house formerly occupied by a Victorian-era female archaeologist: astronomical.

Mouth dry, I ask her, "Do you honestly believe in stuff like that?"

"Well," Trudy whispers, pressing her lips against my ear, "I'm beginning to believe that wishes come true. Same thing, right?"

Fingers linked, I wander with her back toward the library, unspeaking, listening to the roar of the river, the rush of the cars, the thud of my heart. Trudy pulls me into the library building behind her, neatly seats herself at her desk, crosses her legs, and regards me seriously, her hands templed beneath her chin. "Now, down to business, Ms. Strange." She opens a drawer and pulls out a manila folder. "This is for you."

I take the folder from her and smile at the handwritten label: *Ghost Team Investigation: Cascade Avenue Victorian House, Trudy's Report.* Flipping open the cover, I find a couple of typewritten pages and a post-it note stuck to the back of the folder. *Who you gonna call?* is written on it in sparkly purple ink, along with a phone number. "Your cell?"

"Figured we'd reached that stage. It's sweet and old-fashioned doing the "next time we run into each other" routine, but I'd like to have the option of sending you lewd texts and inappropriate photos when the mood strikes. Unless you'd object to—"

"No objections here. But fair is fair." I lean over Trudy's desk, pick up a pen and reach for her hand, writing my cell number on her palm as she watches me with a raised brow, blonde waves gleaming like honey.

"Nice penmanship."

"Thanks. I got an award for my cursive in second grade."

"So you've always been good with your hands..."

I laugh softly, and when I draw back, she regards her palm, head tilted to one side. "You know, they say seeing ghosts together is a bonding experience."

I chuckle again, watching her fondly. "Do they?"

"Mm. So next time we have...some privacy"— she glances at the patrons in the library with a pout—"I think we'll feel closer than ever before. And, technically, this is the *longest* relationship I've had in my life. We've been dating since we were fourteen, after all. Even if it was only in my imagination."

I chuckle a little, blushing. "You make me sound like Puff the Magic Dragon."

"What do you mean?"

"Like your imaginary friend."

"Well... Lucky me—I don't have to imagine you anymore."

A young man in a blue button-down shirt and

jeans suddenly appears beside me, says to Trudy, "Sorry. I just had a question about some books I need for a class. Do you have a second, or should I come back later?"

"Oh, I have to get back to the house." I shrug, smiling. "It's a renovation day, and I'd feel guilty if I let poor Cordelia do all of the dirty work by herself."

Trudy bends over her desk, expertly flicking the top button of her dress so that it comes undone, revealing the lace edge of her black bra. "Wish I could help you with that dirty work, Alex."

My blush deepens as the man glances between the two of us, his freckled cheeks as round and red as an apple. "Um, really, I could come back—" he stammers.

"No, no, I should go." I hold Trudy's folder against my chest and take a couple of steps backward. "See you soon?"

She holds up her palm, scrawled with my cell phone number. "I'll be in touch, Puff. Oh, and make sure to read that report tonight!"

Still reeling from the revelations of the afternoon, I wave goodbye and hurry out of the library, into the warm midday sun. My brain is electrified, too scattered to walk home right away, so I run over to the park and sit down on a bench beside the river. For a long moment, I watch the peaked waves, the seagulls diving, the ducks floating ever closer to the falls. Slowly my blood pressure levels out, soothed by the white noise of the water.

When I woke up this morning, the first thought that took shape in my mind wasn't, oddly enough, related to the Ghost Team or the apparitions.

All I could think of, imagine, visualize was

Trudy in that club with Ruby...and what may or may not have happened afterward.

Still, when I was in her company today, I couldn't bring myself to ask her how her night had gone. I couldn't bear to know; I cringed at the risk of revealing my own insecurities...

But, *damn*, my mind won't stop looping.

Sighing, I open the folder across my lap and begin to read.

Trudy's account is straightforward, a concise description of the night's investigation. Of course, she made no mention of our kissing in the entryway, or of Ruby's insinuations, but at the very end, she scribbled a message in the same sparkly purple ink from the post-it note.

*Tiger,*

*We're on to something big here. I can feel it. Weird thing is, I keep dreaming about Elizabeth. Never Victoria, only Bess. (And, well, sometimes you, but that's off-topic...and unfit for print. Remind me to tell you about it later...)*

*Let's put our heads together, Sherlock Holmes and Watson-style (always suspected they had a thing for each other; didn't you?) and figure it all out. Want to meet at my place tomorrow night, say six-ish? 333 Fourteenth Street, Apartment 6.*

*Bit of a drive, but I'll make it worth your while. Cross my heart.*

*T.*

❧

142

I roll over in bed, drained but sleepless after an evening of sawing and sanding, hammering and vacuuming. I scrubbed those fireplace stones until they gleamed. Cordelia ordered a pizza for dinner, because neither of us was functional enough to cook, but that was hours ago, and now my stomach is rumbling again.

I never realized how many calories manual labor can burn. I'm used to working in the sun on my dig sites, but none of that exertion compares to what I've been putting my body through since Cordelia arrived. My wrists hurt. My knees hurt. My shoulders are on fire. For the first time in my life, I feel *old*. Every time I move, my abused joints ache, creaking like the tree branches outside of my bedroom window.

Groaning, I swing my legs over the side of the mattress and stand up. I rake a hand through my tangle of curls, then rub my eyes, squinting at the bloodred wall before me. The remnant of a dream begins to manifest at the farthest edge of my consciousness.

Victoria again. I remember Victoria, remember her pale-colored hair whipping in the wind, casting her face in eerie shadows. She said something to me, held something out to me, and then—

No, *no...*

Then she fell *backwards*, over the Bridal Veil Falls.

Did she slip? I can't recall her slipping, only tipping, screaming—

"God." I grip my forehead, shaking the image, that wail, out of my mind. I never realized how lucky I was, failing to remember my dreams; ever since I came to this house, this town, I've been remembering far too many of them—though, really, it's always the same dream, over and over again. Slightly altered, maybe, but always Victoria, always the falls.

And now...Victoria plummeting over the falls. Gruesome.

I wince, stumbling in the dark. I'm too tired for this. I'm stressed, overwrought. I'm starving. And I have to pee.

Quietly, I tiptoe into the bathroom, flicking on the newly installed chandelier. It's an antique that Cordelia and I were lucky enough to find at a local flea market, hung with strands of crystals and pearls to match the oceanic decor. Cordelia rewired it, just to be safe, and then installed it directly over the sink. During the daytime, the crystals reflect rainbows all over the white shell walls.

I reach up to brush my fingertip over one of the smooth pearls, remembering how Jack told us, as Cordelia was attaching the fixture, that he wanted to explore the ocean someday like Jacques Cousteau, search for sunken treasure. I teased him: *Well, what'll it be, then? The desert or the sea? You have to choose.* And Jack grinned, said, *I'll explore both! And the stars, too!* I ruffled his hair, gave him a hug, promised to take him out on the Maid of the Mist before he heads home to Toronto.

Already, so many fond memories have been born within these walls.

I pause, stiffen, staring at my reflection in the mirror.

Well, it isn't as if I'm growing *fond* of this place, only that we've put so much work into it, and I believe the house ought to go to someone who appreciates our efforts, who notes the little details, the history, the heart.

After I pee, I flush the toilet and start to rise to

wash my hands, but my toe nicks the old conch shell lying beside the bathtub, sending it spinning across the floor. I dive to catch it before it strikes the opposite wall and cracks. Despite my aching muscles, I manage to stop it just in time. But when I pick the shell up and tilt it to one side, something shifts inside of it.

"What the..." I turn the shell over in my hands, inspecting its amber surface for signs of damage. It's in remarkably good shape for a relic of its age— glossy and smooth as glass. Finding nothing, not a scratch, I close one eye and peer into the dark inner whorl.

My breath catches: something glints back at me...almost as if it's winking. "Well, hello there." Heart beating fast—just as it does when I'm about to make a discovery in the field—I rummage around in the medicine cabinet until I find my tweezers; then I squeeze the tweezers between my fingers and catch at the object inside of the shell, drawing it out into the light.

I had expected something metallic, like coins or jewelry, but instead I discover a shiny lock of golden hair, tied with a velvet ribbon around a paper scroll. The edges of the scroll crumble when I touch them. The paper is as fragile as eggshells, browned with age and probably water-damaged, too.

Carefully, I cradle the scroll in my palm and carry it out of the bathroom and downstairs, into the kitchen. There, beneath the bright overhead light, I allow it to roll onto the tabletop while I search for my magnifying glass. I'd loaned it to Jack so that he could inspect a beetle in the garden. Knowing him, he probably became distracted by some other natural wonder—an ant carrying a crumb; a blue jay feather; a sparkly rock—and left it outdoors, buried in the grass.

I move back into the entryway and shiver, chilled all over. Granted, I'm not wearing much, just a tank top and shorts, but I feel as if I've stepped into an underground cave—that cold and that oppressed. I rub at my arms, exhaling a shaky sigh. The house is dark, silent. I hear nothing indoors, nothing outdoors, only my erratic breaths and the complaining floorboards beneath my feet. And, thank God, I don't see any ghosts on the staircase.

So when I hurry through the entryway and slip through the door leading into the backyard, I'm startled by the bright light that greets me there—so startled that I nearly trip over Jack's discarded trowel.

A ghost. At first, that's all I can take in, all my brain can process. Honestly, you'd think I'd be used to this by now, but my body responds as if it's in a supernatural presence for the first time: racing heartbeat, goosebumps, shallow lungs. Soon enough, my tired eyes focus, and I realize that the ghost—hovering just above the weeds—is Victoria. And she's aglow. Her china-smooth skin, her loose hair, the whole length of her, haloed in silver.

She looks like a fallen star.

As my eyes flit up toward the sky and the full moon, the myriad stars, I realize that, weirdly enough, there's a *natural* explanation for Victoria's illumination: she's awash in moonlight. Cascade Avenue may be lined with streetlights, but, like everything on this block, they aren't well-maintained; most of the ones nearest to my house have burnt-out bulbs. Scary for nighttime excursions, but it's an unintended advantage for amateur stargazers. One night, Jack and I were even able to see the Milky Way.

But I can't see the Milky Way tonight, and I have no interest in the stars, because Victoria is a hundred times more beautiful than all of them. I've never seen her so clearly before, not while I was awake; somehow, though, she looks just as she does in my dreams, with her blonde tendrils stirred by the breeze, her sad, pale eyes locked onto mine.

Suddenly, she holds her hand out to me, beckoning me to take it, to touch her.

To *touch* her?

I swallow. Though I've encountered Elizabeth several times now, I never considered touching her. Well, she never invited me to touch her. But I guess I assumed that it wasn't possible, that ghosts are made of mist and memories.

Now, half-frightened, half-thrilled, I reach for Victoria's fingers...but touch nothing, no one, only empty air. Then I fall forward a little, off-balance. "I'm sorry," I stutter, my voice low and hoarse, though I'm not certain what I'm apologizing for. Maybe for that fact that Victoria's eyes darkened when my hand passed through hers, and now her expression, sad but beseeching earlier, is withdrawn, somber. Hopeless.

She looks dimmer; she's beginning to disappear. I feel as if I've failed her, but what does she *want?*

I draw a deep breath into aching lungs. My heart feels heavy, like a dead weight inside of me, struggling with each and every beat. "Victoria, are you... Are you looking for Elizabeth?" The words are whispered, hardly audible; my throat is too dry, too tight.

But Victoria hears me, because she nods her blonde head and gazes wistfully up toward my bedroom window, lifting her arm to point at the curtained panes.

"Okay. Great. Good." I cross my arms over my chest and shiver. "I just... I don't understand. She's in there. In the house. And you're out here. You want to see one another. But if you went inside, or she came outside, you could be together—"

"*No. I—we can't...*"

Instinctively, I take a step back, startled not by the sound of her voice but by the sudden crushing sorrow that forces me to my knees. My bare shins sink into the damp grass as I support myself with my arms, knuckles pressed deep in the cool mud. This isn't my sorrow; it's hers. Victoria's. I experienced the same thing in Elizabeth's presence last night. Apparently ghosts communicate better through emotion than words—maybe too well. I feel as if the grief of the world has taken up residence in my heart.

"You can't?" I force out through gritted teeth, wincing against the pain. "Why? What can I—"

"*Necklace,*" Victoria answers, hissing out the word. Her features are clenched, as if in frustration. With noticeable effort, she adds, "*Locket.*"

"A locket?" I exhale a ragged breath, swiping a tear from my eye. "Okay. Where can I find it? Is it in the house?"

"*Need—*" She flickers, starts to dissipate into small, pixelated teardrops of light.

"No, Victoria. Tell me—"

"*Bess...doesn't...the locket!*" she exclaims, crouching down, curving her hands into claws as she drifts closer, reaching out for me. Her arms move through my body, and I feel the faintest sensation: as if someone is blowing on the back of my neck, or breathing into my ear. It's creepy, unsettling; I recoil, even as I continue to stare into Victoria's fading eyes.

"*Please,*" she whispers, cradling her head in her hands.

A blink, and she's nearly gone, a faceless spiral of silver hovering just above the grass.

"Victoria, how can I *find* the locket?" But it's too late: I'm alone, talking to the darkness. I feel her absence more than I see it. The sorrow left me—in a startling whoosh—along with Victoria's ghost, though my own sorrow quickly occupies the vacated space; I feel more confused than ever. Day by day, reality slips further and further away from me. God, if Lucia, if any of my colleagues could see me now—kneeling in the dirt, convinced that I just communed with a Victorian ghost—they'd have me committed.

*Calm down.*

I have to remind myself that I'm not the only person who has seen ghosts at V. Rex. If I'm crazy, we're *all* crazy. Maybe there's something in the water...

I brush my hands off on my shorts and stand up, despite my knees' painful protests. I'm so spent that I stumble into the house, trip up the stairs and fall into bed—without remembering to look for the magnifying glass or put away the fragile scroll lying on the kitchen table.

# Chapter Eight

"Wake up, Auntie Alex!"

"Hmm?" I squint at the sunlight and roll onto my back. "Jack?" I croak, fumbling for my cell phone on the suitcase bedside table. "What time is it?"

"Seven o'clock!" My nephew sounds as if he just inhaled a balloonful of helium. How can *anyone* be so cheerful at seven in the morning? Or so energetic? He bounces onto the mattress, narrowly avoiding my stomach, and positions his syrup-smeared face two inches away from mine. "We brought you breakfast in bed!" he exclaims, breathing on me sweetly.

"You did?"

"*I* made the orange juice," he boasts, sliding back a little as Cordelia comes into view. She's carrying a wooden tray in her hands and wearing a smile that rivals Jack's in its sunniness.

"Well, it's been years since you've had my secret recipe raspberry pancakes, and Jack squeezes a mean orange. Now, sit up."

Obediently, I raise myself onto my elbows as she rests the tray across my lap: it's laden with pancakes slathered in butter, a carafe of syrup, and a glistening glass of cold orange juice. I shake my head, stunned. "Thank you. This is... Wow. I can't remember the last time I had breakfast in bed."

"You've been sleeping on cots for far too

long," Cordelia chastises me gently. She drags the vanity chair over to the side of the bed and sits down on it. "I figured, it's a cozy, rainy day—perfect for pancakes."

"Yeah." I pick up the fork and smile softly. "Mom always made pancakes for dinner when it rained. I crave them, even now, whenever I hear thunder."

"Me, too."

I meet my sister's warm green-gold eyes. Her brown hair is loose, shining on her shoulders, and she's wearing a Toronto Blue Jays jersey. She, David, and Jack are big baseball fans and try to attend every home game.

Must be nice to share a tradition like that. Baseball games. Raspberry pancakes on rainy days...

Something shifts in my chest as I gaze down at the golden stack on my plate. Wait—I don't even like baseball. My sister and nephew just made me a delicious breakfast, and suddenly I feel like *crying*? God, maybe Victoria's emotions haven't fully sifted out of me yet.

Or maybe... Maybe Niagara Falls has begun to change me, after all. Marie Rosenfeld assured me that it would, but I thought she'd attended one too many New Age lectures. I thought I would leave this experience a little richer but unaltered, with a successfully flipped house under my belt. I thought I'd run back into the field without a single glance over my shoulder.

And I thought my one-night stand with Trudy would be just that—one night—but it's become something else entirely. Something I could have never predicted. Throw a couple of angsty ghosts into the mix, and my life is unrecognizable from its former state of being.  So I guess it makes sense that I might start to feel differently about some things than I did in the past...

I'm just not sure that I like it.

"You look like you're a million miles away. What's up, Alex?" Cordelia prompts me, narrowing her brows.  "Too much butter?"

"No such thing," I say, forcing a smile. "Sorry.  I didn't get much sleep last night.  But I'll be pancake-powered soon enough."

Apparently, my words fell a little flat, because Cordelia is staring at me doubtfully, her lips pursed to one side.  "Did something happen last night?  Did you see another ghost?"

"It was Victoria," Jack replies, as he idly plays with a toy airplane, rolling it back and forth over my comforter's folds.  "Wasn't it, Auntie Alex?"

I lift a brow and shake my head, laughing. "Kid, sometimes you scare me."

"Mommy says that, too."

Cordelia ruffles her son's messy hair with a fond smile.  "Geniuses always scare people.  It's a compliment, sweetheart."

I pour some syrup over my pancakes and then cut into the stack with the side of the fork, taking my first bite.

"Good, right?" Cordelia asks, leaning back in her chair with a self-satisfied smile.

"What can I say?  You're the Canadian Martha Stewart."

Jack pipes up, jumping to his feet on the mattress and nearly toppling my tray: "Try my juice! Try my juice!"

I down a gulp and transform my face into an

exaggerated expression of bliss: "You ought to become a professional orange juice squeezer, Jack."

"Nah. I'm only going to do that part-time." He falls back onto the bed and picks up his plane again.

"When you aren't digging in the desert or scuba-diving in the sea?"

"Uh-huh."

Cordelia and I exchange a smile. "I admire your ambition, sir," I tell Jack, and then I shovel more pancake into my mouth, grinning at my sister appreciatively.

"So you really saw Victoria?"

"Mm. In the backyard. I was—oh!" I drop my fork and sit up straight, eyes widening. "I found this scroll in the bathroom last night—"

"You mean, *this* scroll?" Cordelia reaches behind her back and brandishes the scroll to me. I take it, examine it: it's wrinkled because she was keeping it in her jeans pocket, but it looks fine otherwise. It's still wrapped in velvet ribbon and that golden lock of hair.

"So, Jack and I have spent all morning trying to guess what's written on that thing—"

"All morning?" I laugh. "It's seven a.m.! How long have you guys been up?"

"Early to bed, early to rise. Anyway, *he* thought it might be a treasure map. But *I* thought it had to be a note from your ghost-hunting vixen."

"Trudy?"

She arches a brow. "Well, isn't that her hair?"

"No." I slide my finger over the glossy strands. "It's a similar color, but this stuff is old, Cord. The paper's falling apart. I think it must have belonged to the original owners of V. Rex."

"You mean, Elizabeth?"

"Maybe." I shrug, chewing on my lower lip. "Guess there's only one way to find out." Holding my breath, I slip my finger beneath the knot in the ribbon and tug at it gently. It gives way, fraying at my touch. I catch the lock of hair in my palm as the scroll falls to the bed and begins to loosen.

"What is it? What is it?" Jack asks eagerly, standing on all fours like a puppy. "It's a treasure map, isn't it? Can I help you find it? I have my junior archaeologist kit in my room."

I swallow and touch the edges of the paper. "I should really be wearing gloves for this—"

"Come on, Auntie Alex!"

"Yeah, come on!" Cordelia laughs, looking nearly as excited as Jack. Her green eyes shine bright with curiosity. "I have a revised guess: I think it's a love letter, never sent. You know how repressed those Victorians were."

My sister and my nephew press hard against my shoulders as I unfurl the page centimeter by centimeter, revealing, at last, a single printed line. In faded brown ink, I can make out the words—

*B. Yours forever. Cross my heart. V.*

"That's it?" Jack groans, falling backward on the bed with a sigh. "But I wanted to go on an adventure!"

Mouth dry, I let go of the scroll, allowing it to close in on itself again, and wipe my sweaty palms off on my knees. "Hey, kiddo, we can still go on an adventure," I say hoarsely, coughing into my hand. "I promised you the Maid of the Mist, didn't I?"

"Really? A *ship*? Like a *pirate* ship? Can we

go, Mom?"

Cordelia casts me a disapproving glance and shakes her head. "I don't know. Alex, we were supposed to strip the wallpaper in the living room—"

"Tomorrow."

"But—"

"And, hey, it's already raining, so it won't be a big deal when we get wet on the boat. Might not even have to wear one of those ugly blue ponchos."

"We're wearing the ponchos," Cordelia says, in her Mom-knows-best voice.

"What? So we're going?" Jack shrieks. "Yippee!" And just like a Jack-in-the-box, he springs off of the bed and careens into the hallway— presumably to prepare for his great big "adventure."

Predictably, Cordelia clicks her tongue and gives me a green-eyed glare. "Jack and I will be going back to Toronto in a week and—"

"I know. That's why I want to do this. I want to do something fun. Not that injuring myself with nonstop home renovation isn't *fun*—okay, it's not fun." I smile, reach for her hand. "Aside from your lovely company, of course."

"Well...I *could* use a break. I was so tired yesterday that I nearly nail-gunned my ear to the wall. How is that even *possible*?"

"Anything's possible. Remember that time paint dripped off of my brush and right into my mouth? I can still taste it..."

Cord makes a face. Then she flicks her gaze toward the mysterious letter lying between us. "So what do you make of that?"

"Don't ask me yet."

"What?"

I shake my head, close my eyes for a long moment. My heart is skipping beats, and my temples are beginning to throb. "I'm still trying to piece it together. Last night, Victoria told me that I have to find a locket. She told me that she wants to be with Elizabeth, but—"

"Wait. You think she wrote this letter to Elizabeth—er, Bess? B and V, Bess and Victoria? You think they were in *love*?"

I pause, considering. It isn't scientific to guess. I should take the letter to a lab, have someone date it, before I jump to any conclusions. After all, B and V could be Becky and Vincent, or Boris and Vladimir, an endless combination of names. The letters might refer to nicknames, rather than first names, making identification difficult. Without more data, the possibilities are immeasurable, astronomical.

Maybe some squatters snuck into the house during its vacancy and shoved the letter into the shell—as an earnest gesture or as a joke. There's no question that the letter is old, but how old? I don't know, can't know... I don't even know if it was ever read by its intended recipient.

Still, I tell Cordelia, "Yeah. I think Victoria wrote this letter to Bess. And...yeah, I think they were in love." A rush of cold air blasts around the room after I pronounce the word *love*, and Cordelia stands up, startled.

"Did you feel that?" she asks, looking toward every corner of the room. "Do you think—"

"It's Elizabeth." My voice is low, husky. I gaze down at my nearly finished plate of pancakes and swallow. "Maybe she was here all along."

"Listening?" Cordelia cringes.

"Well, what else does she have to do?" I smile slightly as a cool gust grazes against my cheek, causing my hair to lift from my neck. "All she can do is listen. And wait."

"Wait for *what*? You're creeping me out, Alex."

"I'm creeping myself out."

"Okay, I have an idea." Seating herself back in the chair, Cordelia wraps her arms around her knees and leans forward, staring hard into my eyes. "Now, don't say no right away. Think about it first." She draws in a deep breath. "How about a séance?"

"A séance? You think we should—"

"Yeah! I mean, no, the thought terrifies me. Deeply. But think about it. These ghosts seem to have trouble communicating with us. Understandable, considering they're inhabiting the ethereal plane. Or the spirit world. Whatever. They're...*elsewhere*.

"But a séance would make it easier for them, wouldn't it? Bridge the gap? That way, through a medium, they could tell us what we need to do, how we can help them—"

"I don't know." My stomach twists into a series of knots, but another gust brushes over my face, my mouth, as gentle and lingering as a lover's kiss. God, does Elizabeth *want* us to have a séance? Do people even do séances anymore? How am I supposed to arrange one? Why am I even considering this?

But I know why, have known for some time now.

Elizabeth and Victoria are lost, or trapped, or suffering, and if we don't help them, they'll stay that way—possibly forever. I can't imagine what it's like to be in their place, but I do know what it's like to feel soul-searing grief, to feel such deep anguish that you don't know if you'll survive it, don't know if you want to survive it.

They're in torment, Elizabeth and Victoria both, and it would be too cruel to ignore that pain. It would be unforgivable.

I would never forgive myself if I abandoned them now.

They trusted us enough to reach out, to expose their vulnerabilities; the least we can do is attempt to ease their suffering. And if our trying involves holding a séance in the living room, I guess I'd better start searching eBay for a crystal ball.

⚜

"You're wet."

"It's raining. And we took Jack on the Maid of the Mist."

"His first time?"

I nod, shaking off my umbrella and handing it to Trudy, who tosses it into the hallway closet with a lazy smile. "Seems like the boat got closer to the falls when I was a kid—" I begin, but then Trudy's kissing me, pressing me hard against the art nouveau-style mirror attached to the hot pink-painted wall. My mouth is wet from the mist and the rain, and soon Trudy's mouth is wet, too, as she licks my neck, nips at my ears...

"I didn't mean to interrupt you, tiger, but we're short on time." She unsnaps my henley and kisses the rise of my breasts.

"Short on time?" I ask her, breathing hard.

"The gang's coming over."

"You mean—"

The *ding* of the doorbell cuts me off and causes Trudy to groan, her forehead falling softly against mine. "I told them seven-o'clock," she whispers. "It's *six*-o'clock. I'm sorry, Alex. It's just—they really wanted to give you their reports in person, so..." She swings open the door—and gapes. "Oh. Hi, Ruby. Where are the others?"

"They aren't coming," Ruby says, shoving past Trudy and moving into the apartment, while, frowning, I begin to snap up my shirt. "Were you two in the middle of something? Comparing...*notes*?"

Trudy huffs. "If you're only here to make snide remarks—"

"I'm here to drop off these." She flings a pile of folders onto a side table and angles me a sinister stare. But after a moment, she deflates: her shoulders sink, and she shrinks by about an inch, raking a hand through her spiky white hair. "Okay, look. I...I came here to fight."

"To *fight*?" Trudy's jaw drops. "Seriously? What—"

"Tru, I came here because I'm upset. Because I miss you. Because I thought I could win you back. But the fact is..." Her face crumples. "I know I just need to let you go."

"Ruby..."

"I've known you for years, Tru, and I've never seen you as happy as you've been since you met Alex. God, it *guts* me. But I love you, and I can't ask you to give this up. That would be...wrong. Damn it." She smiles sadly, glancing between us. "Problem is, you don't look at me like you look at her. Never have."

Trudy, pale and shocked, places a hesitant

hand on Ruby's shoulder. "Honey. Come on. Sit down, and we can—"

"No. I'll be okay. Honestly. I guess I never realized how much I—you know, I try to act all tough, but—oh, never mind." She swipes a hand across her eyes and shakes her head, squaring her shoulders. "I knew it was over when we went to the Manic Pixie Nightmare Girls show. You used to hang all over me, and suddenly it was like you wouldn't even *touch* me. You apologized when our shoulders bumped together, for God's sake."

She shoves her hands into her jeans pockets, sullen. "I only have myself to blame. I didn't try hard enough. I didn't ever let you in, not really. But even if I had, I think... I think you two would have found each other in the end."

Trudy exhales a shaky breath. Then she casts me a knowing glance and a soft, trembling smile. "I think we would have, too," she agrees, reaching for my hand, entwining her fingers with mine.

"Yeah." Ruby ducks her head, staring down at her thick-heeled boots. "So...those're the reports. I sent you the email from the group address. Sorry. Don't blame them. Anyway, I should go."

"Wait." Still gripping my hand, Trudy grabs Ruby's jacket lapel and draws her toward her, says, "You can't just *go*. Not after everything we've been through together." She lowers her voice, and there's a catch in her throat when she says, "All love stories should end with a kiss."

Then Trudy stands on her tiptoes and touches her lips to Ruby's lips—lightly, lingeringly—and I watch as a single tear slips from the corner of Ruby's eye. "You'll always be here," Trudy tells her, drawing back and pressing a fist to her heart.

Ruby copies the gesture, though her fist looks tighter, and she pounds it hard against her chest, too hard. "Take care of her, Alex," she forces out, before spinning around and crossing the threshold, closing the door behind her with a bone-rattling slam.

"Oh, my God." Trudy sinks against me; I catch her, holding her up and guiding her toward the black velvet living room sofa. "Oh, my God. I'm so sorry, Alex. I just—I didn't expect that. Ruby and I have been drifting apart for months, long before I met you. But we kept having sex because—well, we both love sex. And we see each other all the time because of our Ghost Team work. We called one another FWBs. I had no idea that she felt—I mean, I would have never—oh, that was awful. I'm so sorry." She sinks down onto the couch, cradling her blonde head in her hands.

"Don't apologize." I sit down beside her and sling my arm around her shoulders; she buries her face against my neck, crying quietly.

"But I didn't want you to see me like this—"

"How? Crying?"

"*Weak.*"

"Trudy." I brush her hair back from her forehead, and she looks up at me, her blue-violet eyes wide, endearing, smeared with sparkly eyeshadow and mascara. Her hair is drawn into a side ponytail with a ringlet curl at the end, and she's wearing a pair of black skinny jeans with a purple-and-white polka dotted blouse. She looks adorable, beautiful, sad; my heart aches to look at her, and it aches *not* to look at her.

Oh, my God...

Is this love? My sister described love to me

once as "an addiction, without the guilt." And I can admit, without qualms, that I'm addicted to Trudy Strange: her coyness and her sweetness, her compassion—and her passion. She's the most incredible woman I've ever known. Watching her kiss Ruby sliced me open... I realized in that moment that I can never go back to who I was before Niagara Falls. I can never be that Alex again; it would be an act, a sham. Some things are irreversible.

Like death.

Like...love.

I remember the anguished expression on Victoria's face, on Elizabeth's face. I don't know what happened between them, but I do know that they are pining, long after death, for something they lost. They have no peace; they can't escape the pain, can't rest. I've been stuck in a similar loop ever since my parents died. The only relief I've been able to find has been through casual, detached sex with strangers and friends—but that peace fades quickly, too quickly. To be honest, I'm surprised I haven't taken up drinking or smoking or any number of bad habits to fill the void. I'm sure I would have, given time.

With Trudy, though, I step out of myself; I forget my personal tragedies and wake up to the present moment. I only need to hear her voice, see her smile, feel her hand in mine, and my mourning veil falls away. The world looks brighter in her company. *I* feel brighter, alive—and real.

I clear my throat and catch a tear coursing from Trudy's eye on my fingertip, watch the way it reflects the light. Then I draw in a deep, quavery breath. "Trudy, if we're going to do this—really do this—we're going to have to get comfortable with...being uncomfortable with each other. It might be hard. We might mess up. Relationships are messy." I offer her a slanted smile. "Or...so I've heard."

She laughs. "Pathetic, isn't it, being relationship virgins at our age?"

"You forget," I whisper, leaning forward to brush my lips against her ear, smiling at the sight of her cupcake-shaped earring. "We've been dating since we were fourteen. Call me corny, but maybe we were both just waiting—"

"—for you to buy a haunted house and stumble up to my reference desk?" I feel her mouth curve against my cheek. "But, sure, I'll buy that, Corny. Hell, I'll build a *hotel* on that."

"What, is that Monopoly humor?" I laugh, pulling back to gaze at her with a raised brow.

She tilts her head and pretends to be bashful. "Okay, confession: I'm a Monopoly freak. Sorry. Maybe I should've mentioned that up front." She shrugs, casting me a coy, hooded glance. "I'm always the Scottie dog. And I always *win*."

"That sounds like a challenge, Ms. Strange."

"It *is* a challenge, Ms. Dark. But let's save the games for later. First..." She turns slightly and scoots onto my lap, sliding a hand beneath my shirt. "Let's give this relationship thing a go. Starting with the fun part. What do you say, Alex? Do you wanna get messy with me?"

"Well," I sigh, in a mock-bored tone, "I guess we've got to start somewhere..."

"It is ever so tiresome, isn't it?"

"Nice English accent."

"Thanks, mate. But my French accent is even better," she grins, pulling me toward her for a never-ending, never-long-enough kiss.

♥☙❦❧♥

"...five, six, seven, eight!  Ah, looks like you landed on my Boardwalk, tiger."  Trudy, lying naked on the bed, holds out her hand and wiggles her fingers.  "You owe me  two-thousand smackers.  Pay up or put out."

"Can't I do both?"  I pause in counting my Monopoly dollars to cover Trudy's nipple with my mouth, biting her gently.  Then, grinning, I hand over a wad of pastel cash.

"Player," she laughs.  "I like your style."  She begins to place my money onto her neatly arranged, very thick, piles.  She's beating me by a landslide.  I haven't even bought a house yet, let alone a hotel...

"You know," she says, picking up the pair of dice and rattling them in her hand with a faraway look, "no one ever wants to play Monopoly with me.  Ruby thought it was boring.  All of my librarian friends would rather play Trivial Pursuit.  But I've loved this game since I was a kid.  Truman and I used to play it on the coffee table in our living room."  She smiles to herself, blue-violet eyes fixed on some long-past point in time.  "We laughed ourselves silly making up crazy rules, or going around the board backwards, or stealing money from the bank.  Those are some of my fondest memories of him."

She rolls onto her back then, toppling all of the houses and hotels, and reaches up to tug on my hair.  "Have to admit—I've never played Monopoly with a naked woman before."

"Neither have I."  I grin, lowering myself to fit

my curves over hers. My heart flutters as my skin connects with her warmth, her softness, as my mouth kisses her mouth and her leg moves between mine.

"I think it's exactly what the game was missing. Adds a certain *je ne sais quoi*, no?"

"*Oui*," I chuckle, and then kiss her deeply, heedless of the scattered game pieces and the paper money drifting onto the floor.

It's nearly ten; we made love in Trudy's living room...and then on the kitchen floor after dinner. I told Trudy about the scroll that I found, about my belief that Elizabeth and Victoria were lovers. Then we started to watch an episode of *Ghost Adventures,* but Trudy pretended to hear a "spooky voice" in the bedroom to lure me in there and have her way with me. Not that I offered up any objections...

And now, post-sex, we're playing Monopoly—or...we *were*. God, I should be exhausted by now—sore, sleepy, spent—but I seem to have an endless supply of energy where Trudy's concerned. She crouches over me now, blonde waves tickling my face, and licks my neck, laughing when she finds the top hat game piece tangled in my hair.

And then my cell phone rings. Cordelia's ringtone. She knows I'm on a date with Trudy; she wouldn't call unless she had to, unless something big had happened. Anxiety seizes my gut as I reach for my phone, lying nearby on the bedside table.

I glance at Trudy apologetically. "Sorry. It's my sister."

"Answer, answer." She kisses my shoulder and rises from the bed with a luxuriant stretch; then she steps into the adjoining bathroom and closes the door.

"What's up, Cord?" I sigh into the phone.

"Something wrong?"

"Um." On the other end of the line, Cordelia draws in a deep breath. "I don't know if I'd use the word 'wrong,' but...I'm kind of freaked out and would rather not be here without you right now. Do you think you could—"

"Sure." I glance toward the bathroom door regretfully. Trudy had asked me to stay the night; I was going to text Cordelia to tell her not to wait up for me. But my big sister sounds scared, really scared, so I start to dress, sliding my shirt over my head and searching the room for my carelessly flung panties. "I'll be there soon. I'll have to call a cab. Maybe half an hour?"

"Half an hour," Cordelia repeats, voice shaking. She sounds quiet and small, like a frightened little girl. My heartbeat quickens, and I feel nervous, lightheaded.

"Cord, are you okay? Are you or Jack in danger? What's—"

"No, no, we're fine. Only, you know," she laughs hoarsely, "living in a house haunted by a lively trio of ghosts. Kind of hard to convince yourself that there *isn't* something under the bed when—"

"Wait." I pause, one leg jammed into my khakis; I fall back onto the bed, mouth hanging open as I stare at the lavender wall. "What do you mean, *three* ghosts?" A chill rakes over me, and goosebumps pucker my skin. "There are only two—"

"Well, now there are three. Elizabeth, Victoria, and—according to Jack—a tall, dark, and handsome fellow named Xavier. Well, tall, dark, handsome, and *creepy*. I guess some girls are into that, but I'm not, and when I saw his face in the mirror, I had half a heart attack. I'll probably have the other half waiting for you to come home."

"Oh, my God... Okay, I'm on my way. Wait outside if you have to. Love you!" I drop my phone in my pocket, look down at myself to make sure I'm fully dressed—shirt, pants, socks, shoes—and then knock hurriedly on the bathroom door. "Trudy? I'm so sorry, but I've got to go. A *third* ghost appeared at the house tonight, a man this time, and Cordelia's afraid. Do you want to come with me and—"

"Just let me grab my jumpsuit and my stuff!" she says, opening the door and eagerly racing for her closet. "*Another* ghost? What are we dealing with here? The Hellmouth?"

I grimace. "I hope not. I'm no vampire slayer."

"Of course you aren't." She scoffs as she rifles through filmy blouses and colorful dresses, finally finding her jumpsuit and drawing it out. "Vampires are a myth. *Zombies*, on the other hand—oh, could you hand me my bra? It's right there, draped over the lampshade."

I dangle her lacy lingerie on my finger, and Trudy kisses my hand, knight-in-shining-armor-style, before taking the bra from me and putting it on. "Thanks." With lightning speed, she slides on a new pair of underwear—embroidered with her name on the beribboned waistband—and then she steps into her jumpsuit and zips it up. "All set."

"I'll call a cab—"

"No need. I've got *wheels*, tiger. C'mon. Let me chauffeur you—but I *do* expect a tip." She smiles, wrapping her arms around my waist and drawing me tight against her. "And by *tip*, I mean Monopoly sex—just to be clear."

"Got it."

After Trudy puts on her boots and grabs her ghost-hunting kit, she leads me out of the apartment, to the complex's rain-slick parking lot, where her car, a toy-like aqua blue Aveo, awaits. Its bumper is plastered with stickers, but I can only make out a few of them in the dark: *Lesbrarian; Librarians do it between the covers; Reading is sexy;* and *Have a nice gay!*

"This is the cutest car I've ever seen." I stand behind it, gaping.

"Her name's Scylla."

"Scylla?"

Trudy shrugs. "Sometimes I geek out over Greek myths. And ghosts. And hot archaeologists who live in haunted houses. Know any?"

I smile at her as I slide into the passenger seat and fasten my seat belt. "Are you sure this thing is fit for the road?" I ask, tapping the window with my knuckles. "It feels as if it's made of plastic."

"It *is* made of plastic. The best things in life are made out of plastic. Tupperware. Creepy dolls. Monopoly hotels." Trudy begins to back out, glancing over her shoulder. "And good old Scylla. Don't worry. She may not be Ecto-1, but she'll get us to V. Rex as well as any snooty *non*-plastic car could. No, better! Because she's adorable."

"So are you," I laugh, sliding my hand onto her knee. And then, tires screeching through puddles, we're on our way...

# Chapter Nine

Cordelia is sitting on the doorstep when we pull up to the house, a sleeping Jack lying across her lap. She waves weakly at us, attempts a smile, but her eyes are shadowed, and when she coughs into her hand, she sounds sick, hoarse. I take in her bitten-off nails, her red, swollen face...

Panicked, I close my car door and hurry to her side, seating myself on the concrete beside her. "Cord. We got here as quickly as we could. Can you tell me what happened now? Do you want us to take you somewhere else? A hotel?" I rest a hand on her shoulder and peer closely at her, worry wrinkling my brow. "What do you need?"

Cordelia whispers, "A hammer."

"A hammer?" I frown and cast Trudy an anxious glance. She bites her lip, taking a step closer. "What do you need a hammer for?"

"We have to smash the mirrors. All of them." My sister turns to me, her green eyes flashing yellow beneath the newly installed porch light. "He's in the mirrors. I think...he's been watching us through the mirrors."

I don't know how to react to that, so I remain frozen by her side, trying—or, rather, struggling—to absorb her words. Frankly, I don't *want* to absorb her words. The hairs on the back of my neck have begun to rise. "He?" I ask quietly. "You mean Xavier." Speaking the name aloud triggers a dormant memory in me: where have I heard it before? I think hard but can't summon the answer, though I can feel it on the edge of my consciousness, poised to break through...

Agitated, Cordelia looks away from me, says, "I think there's a hammer in the kitchen. I used it last night to fix that wobbly shelf in the pantry."

"Okay." I swallow, patting her softly on the back, and then smoothing a loose strand of brown hair out of her eyes. "Listen, you and Jack stay here. Trudy and I will take care of this. Just stay here, Cord. You'll be safe here."

"Alex." She looks at me with a slanted frown, outwardly calm—though her eyes are as wide as moons. "I may be acting weird right now, but don't worry. I'm not in shock or anything. It's just...remember that movie we watched when you were in fourth grade? Mom got so mad at me for letting you see it. It was about some dead guy who came out of people's mirrors to attack them."

I bow my head, smile mirthlessly. "Yeah. I remember. I refused to brush my teeth in front of a mirror for a week after we saw it."

"Me, too. And now I might have to give up mirrors altogether." Her voice breaks on her final words. She exhales heavily and combs her fingers through Jack's unruly curls, and when she glances back up at me, her eyes are brimming with tears. "He knew my name. Jack's name. *Your* name. He's been here all along."

"Oh, my God," Trudy whispers, cupping her hands around her face. She's standing a few feet away from us; her pink jumpsuit seems to glow in the dark, but her cheeks are pale, drained. I watch as she swallows and draws in a deep breath. "Alex, should I call the others?"

I shake my head, shrugging. "Do you think they could help? I mean, have you ever dealt with anything like this before?"

"No. Never."

"Right." I nod, exhaling through my nose as I rise—shakily—to my feet. "Then there's no reason to wake them up. Two women are perfectly capable of smashing some mirrors," I assert, with one hundred— no, *two* hundred—percent more confidence than I feel. Instinctively, I begin to count up the mirrors in the house, multiplying them by seven years' bad luck each...

God, *stop*. I'm not superstitious, and I need a clear mind to confront this...man, ghost, dark spirit— whatever it is—head on.

Leaving Cordelia and Jack outside, Trudy and I, hand in hand, walk into the house and close the door soundly behind us, making a beeline for the kitchen— where, luckily, there's aren't any mirrors at all. I stick my head into the pantry and find Cordelia's hammer on the floor, while Trudy grabs a log from the basket by the fireplace.

"Should we split up?" she asks. "I could break the mirror in the bathroom while you smash the one in your bedroom. Then we'll tackle the smaller ones together."

"Wow, this really is a horror movie, isn't it?" I smile weakly, leaning against the brick wall. The exhaustion has finally hit me—at exactly the wrong time and place. I have to be alert and quick on my feet, not spaghetti-limbed and slouchy. I sigh, straighten, but my breaths are still ragged, and my muscles ache.

"It's never a good idea when the characters split up in horror movies," I begin quietly, "but I think you're right. The faster we can contain this guy, the better. Who knows what he's capable of?"

Trudy shivers, clutching her mirror-breaking log with white fingers. "I don't want to know."

"Me, either. Okay. We can do this. Right?"

"I... Sure? Sure. I think. Maybe?"

"Come on. I'll race you upstairs."

But we don't race so much as amble, climbing the staircase in slow, reluctant steps, two women loath to face off with an invasive, supernatural Peeping Tom. I muse, distractedly, that there aren't any mirrors in the entryway of the house, so at least this Xavier couldn't have watched Trudy and me having sex...

Probably.

I hope.

My mouth, my throat are as dry as sand.

We walk the length of the hallway, our heels clip-clopping over the floorboards, and then we pause on the thresholds of our adjacent rooms. Both doors are open, but the lights are off.

"Let's count to five," Trudy says, nodding at me as she draws in a gulp of air. "One, two..."

"...three, four..."

"Five," we say together—and I plunge into the darkness of the bedroom, fumbling for the light switch...and immediately regretting turning on the overhead chandelier.

Elizabeth is here.

She looks afraid, petrified.

And she's not alone.

All I can make sense of at first is Elizabeth's shape, sheathed in her usual black dress, and a detached pair of arms—reaching for her, grabbing for her. The arms aren't connected to a body; they're nearly transparent, and they're extending out of the vanity mirror. I flash-back to that awful movie Cordelia and I watched when we were kids. Wasn't there a scene just like this? A pair of arms came through a mirror and tried to strangle a woman who was standing nearby...

I edge along the wall, backing up toward my bed, in order to get a better view of the drama before me. And I can see him—Xavier—*behind* the mirror, though only his arms have materialized in three dimensions. Cordelia's description of him was accurate enough, I guess: he looks to be tall, with dark hair, black eyes, and his features could be construed as handsome. Could be...if he weren't wearing that vile expression—forehead creased, eyes squinting, teeth clenched but bared between his lips. He intends violence, and Elizabeth is struggling against him. Somehow, without touching her, he's pulling her closer, despite her frantic efforts to escape. Now his fingers are mere inches from her throat...

"Stop!" I shout, startling myself and Elizabeth, though the man in the mirror doesn't pause in his endeavor, only sneers slightly and whispers, "Hello, Alex."

My blood runs cold.

I can't move.

I can scarcely *breathe*.

This isn't fear; this is real: Xavier is doing something to me, disabling me, holding me off. A low growl builds in my throat, and I concentrate all of my will on moving. I *have* to move. I *have* to help Elizabeth—

And suddenly, I stumble forward, banging my

knee against the poster of the bed. But I keep running, lifting the hammer high above my head and hitting it against Xavier's face with a deafening *crack*.

He winks out, like a television that's just been turned off. All that remains in the antique frame are broken shards, broken reflections of my face, Elizabeth's face.

I turn toward her, step closer to her, but she's sobbing, shaking her head, growing dimmer with each passing second. "Who is Xavier?" I ask her desperately, dropping the hammer to the floor. "Is he hurting you? Is he the one keeping you trapped here? And Victoria, too?"

Elizabeth, fully see-through now, focuses on me, nods her dark head once, twice.

"If we smash the mirrors, will he go away? Is that all we have to do?"

"*He*—" Elizabeth begins, sounding distant and pained. She opens her mouth to say something else, but before she can utter another word, her form dissipates, comes apart, vanishes. And that's when I feel Trudy by my side.

Without even glancing at her, I reach for her hand, grateful for the warmth of her presence; my bedroom is so cold, and the air crackles with ozone, with emotion, with tension. I can't help looking toward the mirror again, terrified that a pair of black eyes might be staring out at us through the remaining shards.

But the mirror is empty. The room is empty.

Silent, Trudy and I step out into the hallway, where I collapse in her arms.

❧✦☙

I feel as if I might never sleep again.

When I was only sharing the house with the ghosts of Elizabeth Patton and Victoria Richards, I felt, for the most part, at ease and unafraid. Somehow, I knew that there was nothing to fear from either of them, and Cordelia told me that she felt the same way.

But the presence of Xavier changes everything.

Now we're creeped out if we have to venture anywhere in the house alone—including the bathroom, even though Trudy broke that mirror into atom-size pieces. We smashed *all* of the mirrors in the house—the one over the fireplace in the salon, the cheap full-length mirror from Target in Cordelia and Jack's bedroom, the compact mirror in Trudy's purse. We even disconnected the light fixture in the master bedroom because it used tiny dangling mirrors as decorative elements. It's currently sitting out on the curb with a *FREE* sign lying beside it.

Now, at nine o'clock in the morning on a Saturday, Trudy, Cordelia and I are still wide awake, seated around the kitchen table and downing inky cups of coffee from Bean Power. Jack is playing in the backyard. He saw Xavier last night, too, but—blessed with the unworried brain of a child—he seems to have forgotten about it, or at least moved on to more interesting topics. He's become convinced that there's treasure buried somewhere around the house, so he's digging up the yard with his trowel. I need to have landscapers create a new lawn back there, anyway, so I told him he's free to dig as much as he likes. Besides, the three of us are far too rattled; I'd rather he were outside, apart from us, than subjected to our insomnia-producing fears.

I take a bitter sip of my coffee, glance at Cordelia, then at Trudy, and—resigned—nod my head. "Remember when you suggested a séance yesterday, Cord?" I ask her huskily, rubbing a hand over my eyes.

My sister stares at me above the rim of her mug. "What are you thinking, Alex?" Her voice is thin, strained.

"When I bought this place, my agent—Marie—mentioned having gone to a séance. It was only in passing, but I could call her, ask her for some advice. She told me to get in touch if I had any problems with the house...and I'd say this qualifies as a problem." I smile faintly, and Trudy places her hand on top of mine.

"In the meantime," Trudy offers, "I'll go over the Ghost Team's reports myself. We...kind of neglected to do that last night." She smiles at me, a smile that sneaks past my tensed nerves and spikes my heart rate. I blush; Cordelia rolls her eyes. "And I'll give everyone a call, see if they have any ideas, or if they might have had a run-in with Xavier themselves without realizing it."

I duck my head, staring at our fingers entwined. "Sure you want to call Ruby so soon?"

Lifting a brow, Trudy squares her shoulders and offers me another knee-melting smile. Even though her hair is messy, her jumpsuit is wrinkled, and she is just as sleep-deprived as Cordelia and me, she looks beautiful—not to mention strong and brave, two qualities I'm floundering to hold onto. "I'm team leader," she says, "and Ruby's part of the team. We've got to learn to work together all over again. Might as well start now. Besides, with her psychic gifts, she might have had some impression from Xavier that didn't strike her enough to put into her report. Have to cover all the bases."

"Okay." I bite my lip and meet Cordelia's glassy green stare. She's hardly spoken all morning, except to make small talk with Jack as she made breakfast for him, or to reply to direct questions from Trudy and me. I'm worried about her. "How about you, Cord? You know, the offer still stands. If you want to take Jack to a hotel—"

"Alex, I can't abandon you—"

"Hey, I've got plenty of backup here," I smile, inclining my head toward Trudy, who flexes her free arm, striking a Rosie the Riveter pose, "and I'll feel a thousand times more relaxed if I know that you and Jack are happy and safe. Tucked away in a cozy suite, ordering room service and watching HGTV."

"Temptress. You know I can't resist HGTV."

"So are we decided, then? Pick a hotel, any hotel. My treat."

Cordelia sighs, but this time, I think it's a sigh of relief. She folds her arms on the tabletop and rests her chin on top of her hands. "Okay, but only until that...*thing*...is removed from the house. I don't mind the ladies. It's just...*him*." She shivers involuntarily. "We still have work to do—stripping the wallpaper, painting, getting the backyard into shape. And we haven't touched the basement or the attic."

"There'll be time for all of that."

"If you say so."

"I *do* say so. Now go round up your wayward child and start stuffing your suitcases."

Cord smiles weakly. Then she reaches out to squeeze my and Trudy's hands. "Be careful, guys.

Promise me?"

"Cross my heart." Trudy makes an $X$ over her chest, smiling broadly.

I stare at her and tilt my head, remembering Victoria's letter to Bess: *Yours forever. Cross my heart.* When Trudy turns her smile toward me, I'm a little startled to note how much she resembles Victoria. I suppose I noticed it before, subconsciously. That's why I thought Victoria's ghost was so stunning when I encountered her in the backyard; she reminded me of Trudy. They aren't identical, of course, but there's something about Trudy's mannerisms that resemble Victoria's, and they both have that glorious yellow hair...

After Cordelia leaves the room to gather her son and their belongings, I grip my head in my hands for a moment, suddenly overwhelmed by the task before us—and by fatigue.

"You should sleep," Trudy says softly, pressing her lips to the corner of my mouth. "I'll reserve the hotel room for Cordelia and then watch over you while you're in bed. Do you have any books that I could read? Oh! How about those biographies on the Patton family?"

"You're interested in the Patton family?"

"Well, now I am. Don't forget—I'm a librarian, tiger. Knowledge is like eating cupcakes for me. And I once ate a dozen cupcakes *in one sitting.*"

"That's a lot of cupcakes."

"I'm part-hummingbird."

"Makes sense." I yawn; then I lean back in my chair and regard her fondly. "If you really wouldn't mind—"

"It would be my pleasure." She smooths my

hair back from my forehead. "You need rest. And after you've slept, we'll make a solid game plan to deal with this Xavier quandary. Sounds like a trashy sci-fi movie, doesn't it? The Xavier Quandary."

My head—which feels as heavy as a bowling ball—nods of its own accord.

"All right, then, Non-Sleeping Beauty, let's get you upstairs. And show me where the books are. Wait a second—aren't they overdue by now?"

"Um..." I grin at her sheepishly. "I was hoping you'd show me some nepotism, maybe waive the fines."

She stands and helps me to my feet, kissing me deeply as I rise up beside her. "Oh, I'll waive your fines, Alex. And by *waive your fines*, I mean waive your fines—and then I'll lock you in the Niagara Falls collection room with me. As punishment." Her eyes twinkle mischievously.

"If you're sure those glass cases can withstand another round."

She grins, guiding me up the staircase. When we reach Cordelia's room, Trudy sticks her head through the doorway, says, "I'll be back in a sec to help you find a place to stay. Just have to put poor Alex to bed first."

"Good. Make sure she gets four hours of sleep, at least."

"Aiming for eight, but we'll see how it goes. She's a stubborn one."

"You're telling me..."

"Hey," I chuckle, "I *am* right here. And I am not stubborn—"

Trudy and Cordelia share a knowing smile.

"Sure you aren't, little sis," Cord grins. "Now

get in that bedroom and zonk out—no arguments."

"I'm going, I'm going..."

Trudy makes a show of tucking me into bed: fluffing the pillow first, and then drawing back the comforter and sheet so that I can slide right in. I have to admit: it feels *amazing* to be lying down on something soft after being tense all night long. Trudy covers me up with the blankets—and then covers me over with her warm length, pressing me into the mattress as she steals a long, lovely kiss.

"Sweet dreams, Alex. I'll be back in a few minutes."

"The books are on the vanity—but watch out for broken glass."

Her mouth slants to one side. "Maybe I'll do a little tidying up around here, too."

"No, you need sleep just as much as I do—"

"I'm too wired to sleep, honestly. I mean, this is the kind of thing I've dreamed about all of my life."

"An evil entity who pops out of mirrors? You've dreamed of that?" I ask, narrowing my brows.

"No, silly." Trudy kisses me again, harder this time, her breasts against my breasts, her knee bent between my legs and applying gentle pressure. "I've dreamed of a woman who I can't stop thinking about, who fills my stomach with butterflies, who inspires me to be better, to be braver, and to...allow myself to be loved."

I stare at her with wide eyes. "Oh," I whisper.

"You have no idea how much you affect people, do you?"

"I know how much you affect me."

"Tell me how much."

I draw my arm out from beneath the comforter to rest my hand against the side of her cheek. "So much that it scares me. God, *too* much, but I always want more."

"You'll get more, tiger. Lots more," she promises in a low, husky voice, kissing the tip of my nose. Then she slides off of me and pauses beside the door frame. "Dream of me. I'll be back soon."

I roll over onto my side and close my eyes, trying to still my whirling thoughts. Trying to push away the image of those arms reaching for Elizabeth. Trying to forget the arrogant confidence of Xavier's voice when he spoke my name. Right here. In this room.

Curling up into the fetal position, I cocoon the covers more tightly around me and draw in several deep breaths, willing sleep to come. It does, but it brings nightmares with it: again, Victoria standing on the edge of the Bridal Veil Falls—and this time, there's another figure standing beside her. A man dressed in black, with black hair and black eyes.

Xavier glances at me wickedly. And then he pushes Victoria, sending her plummeting to her death.

# Chapter Ten

I blink and sit up, rubbing my eyes blearily.

"Good evening, beautiful." Trudy is lying beside me on her stomach, a library book propped up on the pillow. She slides onto her side and smiles up at me lazily. "Feel better?"

"What time is it?"

"Nearly six."

"Six! And you've been here all alone—"

"It's okay. Aside from some cold spots and an orb in the backyard—far away, over that pond—I haven't experienced anything too weird. Although..."

I stare at her worriedly. "Although what?"

"Well, I went into the bathroom to pee, and when I washed my hands—so, the sink was plugged. I didn't realize that at first. The water started to fill the bowl, and I thought I saw..." She pauses, gazing up at me uncertainly. "Do you really want me to tell you?"

"No." I smile, caressing her knee. She's changed out of her jumpsuit and is wearing only her panties and my NYU tank top. "But tell me, anyway."

"Well, I thought I saw a man's face."

"Oh, my God—"

"No, don't freak out. Nothing happened. I pulled out the plug, and he whirled away, along with the water."

"But, Trudy, that might mean that Xavier can

inhabit any reflective surface. Water. Glass. Anything shiny."

"It *might* mean that. But it also might not mean anything. My eyes could have been playing tricks on me. I haven't slept, and I'm kind of *expecting* to see a ghost at every turn, so... I'm not sure that I'm a reliable witness. But never mind that now. I have something more important to tell you." She sits up beside me, bringing the book onto her lap, and her blue-violet eyes latch onto mine. "I know who Xavier is, Alex."

"You do? How——"

"Look." She swings the book toward me and points to a sentence near the top of the page:

*A private man, Godrick Patton kept a small household. According to records found in his Cascade Avenue residence, he had only two servants: a cook named Anne Ballard and a personal valet, Xavier Manderson, who often accompanied Godrick on his voyages.*

I read over the paragraph again, mentally kicking myself for forgetting the name of Godrick's valet. "I knew *Xavier* sounded familiar." I sigh and lean back against the headboard. "He was mentioned in another book that I skimmed through, but his existence totally slipped my mind. Not that remembering him would have made any difference. And we still don't know how to get rid of him."

"No, but I read through the Team's reports and made a couple of calls. Back in Puerto Rico, Marisol dealt with something like this—a malevolent spirit. She participated in a séance to persuade the spirit to leave."

"And did it?"

Trudy scoots back beside me, pressing her shoulder against mine. "No. But through the séance, they found out what the spirit wanted. Apparently it was angry that the house it had once lived in had been renovated. It wanted everything put back to the way it was before."

I lift a brow and laugh weakly. "Do you think that's what *Xavier* wants?"

"Doubt it. This was never his house. Why would he care about the changes you've made? Though house renovation has been known to awaken dormant spirits. It's like they're in stasis until they hear the power saws and jackhammers. But listen to this—oh, wait. I have a prop." Trudy reaches beneath the pillow behind her and draws out a pair of black-framed glasses. They have round lenses with horizontal black lines marking the fronts. Trudy puts them on and assumes a faux-serious expression. "Don't laugh. I ordered these from the back of a comic book when I was a kid, and I take them to every ghost hunt—just in case they work."

I stifle a smile. "So...what are they supposed to do? Give you x-ray vision?"

"C'mon, I was *born* with x-ray vision." She eyes my t-shirt-covered chest meaningfully, nodding her approval as she arches a brow. "Anyway, these glasses are called Sixth Sense Specs, and they're supposed to allow me to see into the spirit world."

"Ah. Handy."

"Yeah. Except they've never delivered on their promise. Mostly, I keep them because they help me look like a hot librarian."

"You *are* a hot librarian," I smile at her. "But—don't get me wrong—the glasses are a nice addition. Weird...but nice."

"I hoped you'd like them." She smiles lasciviously and then straddles my lap, leaning forward to trail kisses over my neck. "Mm, what was I saying?"

I bite my lip, stroking my fingers through her hair. "Something about Xavier?"

"Oh, right." She sighs, straightens, and adjusts her glasses, then says, in a news anchor-esque voice: "This just in: Xavier lived in a room in the *attic*. Which means that some of his belongings might still be up there."

I inhale deeply. "And *he* might still be up there."

"True. But what if he has the locket Victoria was talking about? She said she needs that locket. Maybe it's the key to solving this mystery." She wraps her arms around my waist and pulls herself close, so that our stomachs are pressed tightly together. "Up for some excavating, Alex the Archaeologist?" Trudy removes the pair of glasses and places one of its tips into her mouth, lifting a brow as she gazes at me. "I wouldn't mind seeing your skills in action. You've already seen me at my job. It's only fair that I get to watch you at yours."

I smile at her, shrugging. "I'm all for equality. Why don't you get dressed—jumpsuit, shoes; it's dangerous up there—while I give Marie a call, out of the blue, and ask her to help me arrange a séance. That's a normal question for a real estate agent, right?"

"Nope. You're officially weird." She thwacks my thigh. "But get to it!"

While Trudy begins to pull on her jumpsuit, I grab my cell from the bedside table and wander out into the hallway and down the staircase. Marie answers on the second ring.

"Ms. Dark?"

Surprised to be addressed by name, I say, "Hi, Marie. I'm sorry to bother you—"

"It isn't a bother! To be frank, Alex, I have been hoping you would give me a call for weeks. I've been too ashamed to call you myself."

"Ashamed? Of what?"

"Well..." She pauses, and I hear her inhale a deep breath before she says, "I sold you a haunted house."

"You *knew?*"

"Yes, but you'd come so *far*, and I didn't think you—as a scientist—would believe me, anyway, and I just *felt* as if the house was meant for you, so I—oh, but those are only excuses. I should have told you. I did give you some hints, but...I was dishonest, and I apologize. I'm guessing that you want to back out of the contract?"

"What? No. Wait." I stroll across the entryway, to the back door, and step outside; it's a brisk day. Dead leaves crunch beneath my feet. I stare at the dozens of holes Jack dug around the yard and rake a hand back through my sleep-flattened hair. "The remodel is almost done. I'm nearly ready to resell..." I trail off, because my stomach flipped at the word *resell*. I hadn't realized how close I was to saying good-bye to this place.

"Has it been awful?" Marie asks in a hushed tone, as if she's speaking of a taboo subject. "The...disturbances, I mean."

I would hardly call Elizabeth and Victoria "disturbances," but as for Xavier...I have a worse—and less polite—word for him. "Oh," I sigh, "it's been memorable."

"Memorable in a good way?" she asks hopefully.

I consider, crouching down to pick up my magnifying glass, encrusted with dirt, from the grass. "Hard to answer that one. But how did *you* find out the place was haunted?"

"It's been unoccupied for more than a hundred years. I'm an architectural historian, and that piqued my interest. So I did some research on the former owners and explored the nooks and crannies myself. And in so doing...I believe I encountered something otherworldly."

"Can you describe what happened?"

"Of course. Well...I was in Elizabeth Patton's bedroom, admiring the lovely Victorian furniture. They really don't make furniture like that anymore. My dining table is from Ikea, and it looks like something out of a spaceship. But Elizabeth's vanity..." Her voice takes on a dreamy quality. "I could almost imagine her sitting before it, brushing out her long brown hair. And then...I saw..." She pauses, and I try to wait patiently for her to continue, but after a minute, I exhale through my nose, clutching the phone tightly in my hand.

"You saw Elizabeth's ghost?" I prompt her.

"Elizabeth? No. No, I saw a man. In that *mirror.* *H*e faded away, and a ball of light came out of the mirror and sort of...*flew* around the room, as if it were looking for something."

"Xavier," I whisper beneath my breath.

"There were other instances—cold spots, an eerie feeling on the stairs that made me dizzy... Anyway, Ms. Dark, if you aren't calling to challenge the contract, what can I do for you?"

Suddenly, I don't feel quite so embarrassed about my question for Marie. With a slanted smile, I move the phone to my other ear and ask her, "Would you happen to know any mediums willing to perform a séance? I'd pay extra for an immediate appointment, and I will cover any travel expenses, too." I remember Cordelia's haunted expression after her encounter with Xavier, adding grimly, "It's an emergency."

"Oh, dear. I'm sorry to hear things have gotten dire."

"I have some investigators helping me out. I think it's going to be okay..." I *hope*. "But we do need to hire a medium. And I remembered you mentioning something about a séance when we last spoke."

Marie sighs heavily. "Oh, dear," she says again, and I can almost hear her shaking her head, pursing her lips.

To be honest, I'm shocked that she knew about Xavier, but I don't bear her any ill will for selling me a haunted house. She's right: I wouldn't have believed her had she told me. And even if I had, I'm stubborn—as Cordelia and Trudy attested to last night. I would have bought the damn house, anyway, so what difference does it make?

"I do have a medium friend who lives in Lily Dale. It's a bit of a drive, but you might be able to convince her to come to Niagara Falls, if only as a favor to me. Constance Reed is the real deal, I can promise you that."

"Great. Can I have her number?"

Marie reads it off to me, and I repeat it in my head, memorizing it.

"Alex, I truly am sorry—"

"You aren't the one haunting my house,

Marie. Besides, it's a mystery, and mysteries are kind of my thing. Granted, I've never dealt with a mystery like this before, but—"

"I have faith that you're more than equipped for the challenge. You know, Alex, that house had been on the market for years, and not a single person expressed any interest in it. Not even when we were offering it for a *dollar.* No one seemed to notice it at all—until you emailed me. I think that means something. I think *you* were meant to buy this house. To...hmm...save it."

Marie's words set me off-kilter. I tip onto the ground on my bottom, dropping the magnifying glass. Sighing again, I say, "All I want to do right now is make the place feel safe again. And I'm hoping your friend will be able to help me out with that."

"I hope she will, too. Make sure to mention my name. I helped Constance out of a real estate pickle a couple of years back, so she might be feeling grateful. Or guilty. Either way, I'll be thinking of you, Alex."

"Thanks."

"And, again, I'm sorry for withholding information."

"Clear your conscience. I knew this was going to be an adventure when I signed on for it. I couldn't have predicted what kind of an adventure. But I guess that's how life goes."

"You're a wise woman, you know."

"Not sure I deserve that compliment." Trudy steps through the back door, pink-clad, pink-cheeked, a warm smile playing over her lips as she tromps through the weeds and aims for me. "But I think I've gotten a little wiser since I came to town." I hold out my arm, reaching for Trudy's hand. "About some things, at least."

"Good, good. Well, I wish you light and luck—with your ghosts and...everything afterward."

"I appreciate that. Bye, Marie."

"Goodbye, Alex."

Trudy kneels on the ground beside me, leaning forward to kiss my lips. "Ready to brave the deep, dark, dangerous attic?"

"Almost. I got the number for a medium from Marie. Keep your fingers crossed that she'll agree to come to the house."

Trudy crosses her fingers, smiling sweetly. "I'm sure you'll be able to persuade her, tiger. But I don't want to distract you—"

"You *are* very distracting." I tug at her jumpsuit's zipper and press my mouth to a freckle on her breast.

"Oh..." she sighs. But then she moves back from me with a sideways grin. "Let's save dessert for later. It'll give us something to look forward to. How's about I go pay a visit to your resident mice and spiders in the attic while you make that phone call?"

I frown. "I'm not sure if there's a solid floor up there... You'll have to balance on the beams."

"Easy." She scoffs. "I used to be a tightrope walker."

"Really?"

"No. But thanks for believing I could have been. I would have loved circus life. The costumes, the applause—"

"A new woman in every city," I tease her, arching a brow.

She pauses, and her expression shifts, grows somber. She licks her lips and reaches for my hand.

"Alex, I want you to know... I haven't been with any other woman since I met you. I don't *want* to be with anyone else." Her smile is soft, playful but sincere. "And even if I *do* become a tightrope walker and travel the world, I'll tack a photo of you on my caravan wall and kiss it every night—until I can kiss you in person again."

I chuckle lightly, pressing my lips to Trudy's fingers. "And I want *you* to know that if you ever run away and join the circus, I'll be right there by your side. Well..." I glance skyward, pondering. "My balance is laughable, so tightrope-walking is probably out. But maybe I could swallow swords? Dance with fire? Train little dogs to jump through hoops?"

"Better yet—train *ghost* dogs to jump through hoops."

"Ah, you might be on to something there..."

"I can see it now—The Dark and Strange Spectral Circus! Haunting small towns all across America." She shrugs and slants a smile at me. "You know, if they shut down all of the libraries, and if that archaeology thing of yours ever falls through. Always good to have a backup plan."

"Yeah."

Huh.

I've never made a plan—imaginary or otherwise—with any of my love interests before. And Trudy's been talking long term. I have to admit, that used to trigger my fight-or-flight response. But not anymore. Not with her. I just...can't see very far into my future right now. My intention was to sell the house and go back to work—but that would mean leaving Trudy, turning my back on what we've begun to build together.

I'm a realist: I don't think a long-distance relationship would satisfy either of us, not for any lengthy period of time...

So what am I going to do?

"You'll come to the attic after your phone call?"

"Hmm?" I shake my head, summon a smile as Trudy rises to her feet. "Yeah. Of course. Be extra careful, okay? Call out if you need my help."

Once Trudy goes back indoors, I reach again for the magnifying glass and am about to pick it up when my hand stills; I lean closer to peer through the lens. The magnifying glass fell over one of Jack's shallow holes. He'd been digging for treasure but came up empty-handed—though there's a sharp corner sticking out of the mud, its trim unmistakably carved. He might have missed it or mistaken it for a buried stone because it's caked in dirt, but the magnifying glass reveals it to be an old wooden box.

Heart hammering, I tug at the corner of the box, gritting my teeth. This isn't good archaeology, but I don't have any of my tools. A solid minute of pulling loosens the dirt around the box, until finally the earth gives it up, and the square vessel hurtles into the air. I catch it against my chest and then scrape off some of the mud, revealing a metal catch with a tiny broken lock. The lid opens easily, on silent hinges.

I expect bones. Children throughout the ages have buried the bodies of their pets in the backyard, typically in shallow graves. Maybe young Elizabeth had a bird or a mouse who died. Maybe she held a funeral for it, wrapped it in this pretty box, and dug a small hole with her own little trowel.

At first, all I see is more mud and some

pewter-colored beetles.  But I clear the top layer of dirt away and find a single item nestled in a holey fabric bag: not bones but a glass bottle, small enough to fit in a pocket.  It's too plain to be a perfume bottle, though I can't imagine what other purpose it might have served.

I remove the bottle from its fabric casing carefully.  The glass is clear, and the mouth corked, and the interior looks to be empty.  I tease at the cork until it slides loose, and then I sniff at the opening—and recoil.  Whatever this bottle once contained, it was pungent, not perfume and certainly not a food additive.  Maybe it was a particularly foul-smelling medicine.  But why would someone bury a medicine bottle in the ground?

I flip the box over and notice a rusty plate engraved with the initials XM—Xavier Manderson—affixed to the bottom.

Perplexed, I put the bottle back in the box and punch the phone number Marie gave me into my cell phone.  No answer, so I leave a detailed message—probably too detailed—along with the house's address.

Then, box in hand, I stand up and go indoors to join Trudy in the attic.

❧◈❧

Despite Marie's warning that the attic might not be safe, the floor feels sturdy beneath my feet, and it's obvious that the previous occupants used this space quite often—for storage or, judging by the two partially furnished bedrooms, for sleeping.

"I think this room must have been Xavier's," Trudy tells me, aiming her flashing beyond the large entry room—stuffed with trunks and strewn with old, moth-eaten rugs—and into the smaller bedroom of the two. The space is windowless and narrow but kind of cozy. Well, it *might* be cozy if it were clean. As it stands, there are cobwebs stretching across the ceiling and evidence of mice in every corner. A twin-size bed, stripped of its sheets, and a low dresser are the only objects in the room, but there's a picture tacked on one of the bedposts—a photograph. My breath catches in my throat when I realize who the woman in the picture is.

"Elizabeth," Trudy sighs.

I remove the nail affixing the photo to the wooden post and flip the picture over in my hand. In a messy scrawl, someone inked *My Bess* on the back of the image.

"Do you think they were having an affair?"

"Xavier and Elizabeth?" I shake my head, troubled. "I guess they could have been. Maybe. But it just...feels wrong somehow. I told you about Victoria's note to Bess, the one I found in the shell."

Trudy nods, her blonde head tilted to one side. "Love triangle?"

I narrow my gaze at a small hole cut into the opposite wall, at about eye height. Then I place the box that I found in the ground on top of the squat dresser and pull open one of the drawers. Instead of clothing, the drawer is full of faded photographs, an old-fashioned pair of binoculars—or "spyglasses," as Trudy calls them—and a long lock of dark brown hair tied with a bit of string. Trudy reaches past me to pick up the hair and holds it up to my head, frowning.

"Same color as yours. Was probably Elizabeth's."

I take the lock from her and examine it,

frowning, too. It's too long, too thick. When a person gives someone a lock of hair, they typically cut off only a small amount, so that the snip wouldn't be noticeable. But this would be noticeable. I've seen Victorian memorial jewelry and artwork woven from a deceased loved one's hair, and in those instances, large portions of hair were cut off of the head—since the dead, obviously, wouldn't miss it.

A sick feeling forms in the pit of my stomach, and I feel my face go white.

"What is it? What's wrong?"

With shaking fingers, I drop the hair back into the drawer and pick up the pile of photos, tasting bile in the back of my throat. Apparently Xavier was a photographer. These are travel photos, taken on Godrick's dig sites, I assume—sweeping expanses of sand and sky. And Elizabeth is present in nearly every picture. She isn't posing. She isn't aware that her photo is being taken.

Xavier stole her image—just as, I suspect, he stole her hair.

And, worse, he may have stolen her life.

"Here, smell this," I urge Trudy, handing her the small glass bottle. "It was buried in the backyard in this box." I show her Xavier's initials on the metal plate. "XM. There's no mistaking who this belonged to. So what do you think? What do you make of it?"

"Hmm." She uncorks the bottle, sniffs the rim, and her eyes grow distant, thoughtful, a hundred miles away. Then she smells the bottle again. "I know what this is." Her blue-violet gaze clamps onto mine—wide, shining, and unmistakably alarmed. "I...I worked for my father's business the summer after I graduated high school, before I went off to college. Truman was in Canada with some friends. Dad had hoped I'd give up on my college plans and decide to stay on, though he must have known I'd hate it." She grimaces. "When I was a little girl, I used to rescue spiders from the bathroom, carry them outside on the palm of my hand. So the idea of extermination turned my stomach. But I didn't want to disappoint him..." She bites her lip and sighs. "I did disappoint him, anyway, again and again."

I squeeze her shoulder gently.

"Sorry. The point is—" She narrows her eyes at the bottle in her hand. "This is strychnine."

"Strychnine? You mean—"

"Rat poison."

My heart begins to beat at twice its normal pace. "Right. So, if someone buried a bottle that once contained *rat poison* in the backyard—"

"—they were probably covering something up. Like..." Trudy's lips close, and her eyes hold mine. In the harsh light of the flashlights, her features look flat, like they would in a painting, or in a photograph. She shivers. "Alex. I don't want to say it."

"I don't want to, either. But Elizabeth died of a sudden, undiagnosed illness while her father was out of the country, and there's a bottle of strychnine buried in the backyard, and Xavier has all of these voyeuristic photos of Elizabeth in his room..."

"Do you really think he could have—"

"Maybe he found out about Elizabeth's relationship with Victoria. Maybe he was jealous. And maybe—"

"Maybe he poisoned Elizabeth."

"Yeah," I whisper, taking the bottle back from Trudy and dropping it in the box, then wiping my fingers on my t-shirt. "Maybe he did."

A sudden shattering breaks the silence, and we run, heedless of the rumpled rugs and the hovering dark, out of Xavier's bedroom and into the smaller room adjoining it. There are shards of broken mirror all over the dusty floor, along with the heavy mirror frame itself, having tipped over—or having *been* tipped over.

"Oh, God. I only glanced in here earlier. But I saw something draped in fabric and leaning against the wall," Trudy says, kneeling down to pick up one of the shards. "It must have been this mirror. If I'd known it was a mirror—but why would Xavier break it? Alex!" She stumbles backward, flailing to the floor, as a finger, followed by a hand, and then an elongated, misshapen arm emerges from one of the scattered mirror pieces.

I grapple for her, dragging her to her feet and pulling her out of the room, out of reach. But as I'm shutting the door, I notice that the space, which appears to have been used for storage, boasts a bed with unexpectedly frilly coverings...and there are two silky, though moth-eaten, robes draped over the blankets.

Two.

"Trudy, the robes—"

"I know. I saw. Let's get out of here." Trudy pulls me toward the ladder staircase, taking large, leaping steps. "I'm too tired to deal with that Peeping Tom asshole right now. *Run.*"

We trip down the ladder and land on the hallway floor below; with shaking hands, I fold the ladder until it's fastened in place against the ceiling, effectively closing the attic off from the rest of the house: a meaningless gesture, really, because it isn't as if

Xavier is unable to follow us elsewhere. It does seem, though, that the attic might be his domain, given that he lived up there.

Now it's my turn to pore over the library books while an exhausted and shaken Trudy falls to dreams in my bedroom. She's too tired for innuendo as I help her slip out of her jumpsuit. She slides beneath the covers, I plant a kiss on her forehead, then her cheek, then her lips, and moments later, smiling softly, she's fast asleep. On tiptoes, I heft the stack of biographies down to the kitchen, make myself a kettle of tea, and get to work.

I read for an hour, then two, then three. I'm searching for a specific mention of the trip Godrick Patton embarked on just before Elizabeth's death. Why didn't Elizabeth accompany him? And, more importantly, why didn't *Xavier* go with him? Several of the books clearly state that it was Xavier who found Elizabeth's body and telephoned her doctor. Did no one ever suspect foul play? Was Xavier such a model employee? Surely *someone* noticed his fascination with Elizabeth Godrick...

Granted, most of the evidence we've gathered thus far would disintegrate in a court of law, but no court of law will be interested in a late Victorian-era crime, anyway. I'm researching this for Elizabeth's sake, for Victoria's sake. Maybe their spirits just want someone to figure out the truth. Maybe their souls will be set free if—

"Ow!"

I see, too late, that the newly warmed tea kettle on the table has toppled, spilling scalding water over my arm. Ugly red welts swell along my wrist, and hot tears leak from the corners of my eyes as I wince, gritting my teeth against the pain.

But how on earth did that happen? I hadn't even moved, and the table isn't tilted...

Once the shock abates, I stare at my warped reflection in the sideways teapot, watch as my scowl gives way to a too-familiar, sinister grin. "I'd call you a monster, but you'd enjoy that, wouldn't you?" I hiss at Xavier's face, far more angry now than afraid. "Is this how you get off, by hurting women? What did you do to Elizabeth? Did you poison her? Tell me!"

"Alexxx..." his ghostly voice mocks me. "I saw you. I saw you and Truuudy. Just like I saw my Bess with that *whooore*!"

I smack the tea kettle off of the table, sending it clattering to the floor. Then I stand up and toss the kettle into the trash, though it's too hot and begins to melt the garbage bag. With the scent of burning plastic in my nose, I stalk out of the kitchen, climb the stairs, and lower the ladder leading to the attic. "I'm sick of you," I tell the cold, swirling air around me as it teases at my hair, nips at my cheeks. "You chased my sister away, you scared my girlfriend—" I stutter over the word *girlfriend*, unused to the shape of it on my tongue. "And you forced me to smash *antiques*, for God's sake. It's *over*, Xavier."

His laughter swoops around my ears, causing every hair on my body to stand on end—which makes me so furious that my temples begin to pound. I stomp up the rungs and, once I'm standing in the attic, I stomp again into Xavier's room, flinging the drawers open one by one and sending them crashing to the floor. More photographs, stubby candles, some handkerchiefs... And then I reach the bottom drawer, which is larger and deeper than the others. Inside of it is an old-fashioned camera, along with a small black velvet pouch.

Something crashes against the wall; I glance over my shoulder, see what was a small drinking glass broken to smithereens. "Temper tantrum, Xavier?" I whisper, pretending at nonchalance, though I'm beginning to feel nervous—and a little shocked by my own bravado. What exactly am I planning to do here? I don't know how to stop Xavier. The next object he sends flying might connect with my head...

Fingers trembling, I loosen the cord holding the tattered velvet pouch closed and slowly draw out two photographs. At sight of them, my stomach clenches; I'm afraid I might be sick. Something sails past my ear and hits the wall with a thud, but I'm too dizzy to investigate it. Clutching the pouch and the photographs, I run out of the room, back down the ladder, and I careen into my bedroom, where Trudy is sitting up in bed, messy-haired, stricken.

"I heard something—"

"Come on," I tell her breathlessly, reaching for her hand. "We have to get out of the house."

"Now? But I'm not dressed—"

"There's no time. It isn't safe. Hurry—please!"

"I'm coming. Are you okay?"

I nod weakly, pulling her into the hallway. "I'm okay. But—"

Trudy screams as the wall sconce beside her head explodes in a shower of glass. "Run, Alex!"

We fly down the stairs and slide over the polished hardwood until we reach the front door. Maybe I've watched too many horror movies, but I half-suspect the door to be locked, impossible to open, but it gives freely beneath my hand, and then we're outside, panting, washed in moonbeams and the pinprick light of the stars.

And a woman carrying a carpet bag is walking toward us, her thin lips set in a grim line.

"Alex Dark, I presume," she says in a voice that I would describe as early Hollywood-era posh. She sounds cultured, wise, and when she holds out her hands to Trudy and me, they're heavy with rings—pentacles and quartz and silver crescent moons.

I cough; my throat is tight, and my stomach is knotted. "Are you Constance Reed?"

"I am."

I stare, astonished. "But I didn't expect you to—"

"I was in Buffalo for the evening, visiting relatives, and when I listened to your message, I..." Her hazel eyes glint as they drift toward mine. She's an impressive figure, tall, with snow white hair wrapped into a loose bun at the nape of her neck, contrasted starkly with her swooping black brows and long black lashes. Her flowing garments are saturated with every color of twilight. "I cleared my schedule and drove right here. The truth is, Alex, I'd been waiting for your call."

"Waiting?" I narrow my eyes. I'm still breathing hard, still feeling as if I might faint, or vomit, or scream, so I'm having difficulty comprehending this new development. Trudy clings to my arm; there are tiny shards of glass sparkling in her sleep-flattened hair. I begin to pick them out carefully as I clear my throat, ask, "Did Marie tell you she'd given me your number?"

"No, dear. But my spirit guide informed me two days ago that I should be expecting a—and I quote—'call from the dark.' I must admit, that sounded rather sinister, but then I listened to your voicemail, heard you call yourself Alex *Dark,* and I knew that you and I were destined to cross paths. So..." She spreads her arms, decorated with bangle bracelets, and smiles warmly. "Here I am. Shall we begin?"

I glance at Trudy; she smiles weakly and offers me a small shrug, as if to say, "Why not?"

But there's a violent entity loose in my house, and I'm not certain that holding a séance within Xavier's vicinity is going to subdue him. More likely, it will make him more disturbed, more vengeful. I glance at the still-stinging burn on my wrist, swallowing the lump in my throat.

If we do this, one of us might get seriously hurt...

"Ms. Reed—"

"Call me Constance."

"Constance, we—I mean, we just—I'm worried that it's a bad time for this because—"

"*Now* is always the right time," she interrupts me cryptically, though her eyes are twinkling, and her mouth is crooked into a subtle smile. "Relax. I can tell that the two of you are stressed, tired, a little afraid, but you won't have to do a thing. Well, aside from focusing your minds and concentrating on the task at hand." With a *swoosh* of skirts, she moves past us slightly and gestures toward the house. "I take it that *this* is the site of the spirit activity?"

"Yeah. But it isn't safe—" Before I can finish my sentence, a windowpane bursts outward from the front hall, spitting glass in our direction. We leap to the side, crouching down to the ground and narrowly avoiding the shards, though broken glass crunches beneath my shoes, and Trudy, barefoot, has to tiptoe to the grass to avoid slicing her feet open. I offer Constance a shaky, slanted smile. "Like I said, it isn't safe. He has this thing for glass," I explain quietly.

"He? The entity you mentioned in your voicemail?"

"Mm. He tends to appear in mirrors, reflective surfaces..."

"Of course. A mirror ghost. I've never encountered one, but I'm familiar with the type." With a curt nod of her white head, Constance strides back toward the front door and—bravely—swings it wide. "I don't suppose you have any rooms without mirrors or windows?" she calls back over her shoulder.

"Only in the attic." I curse, wishing that I could take back my words. Because now Constance is going to suggest—

"To the attic, then! Come on now, ladies. We aren't going to let this fellow push us around, are we? There are three of us and only one of him."

"Technically, there are *five* of us," I mutter beneath my breath, shifting my gaze to the front windows, searching them for Elizabeth's face, but she's nowhere to be found. There isn't any sign of Victoria in the yard, either. Xavier has grown powerful in recent days; maybe he's keeping the other ghosts suppressed, muted. Maybe he's done something to restrain them. God, if he has...

The thought causes my hands to clench into fists at my sides. Alternately trembling and fuming, I begin to follow after Constance, who's already climbing the staircase up to the second floor. But I pause before I cross the threshold to cast a glance back to Trudy. She regards me with an oddly blank expression: the face of a doll, fixed in place. My heart clenches in my chest—with fear, with love.

God, I think she's in shock.

"Listen, you don't have to come in." I touch her hair, admiring the way that its yellow waves collect the moonlight. Then I sigh softly, shaking my head. "It's incredibly *stupid* that *I'm* about to go back in this house, but it's *my* house, damn it, and Bess and Victoria need our help, and if I back out now—"

"Alex." Trudy raises a single blonde brow. "Hell will freeze over before I allow you to confront that creeper alone."

Despite the tension in my limbs, despite my contradictory thoughts, a smile steals across my face, and I chuckle quietly, stepping nearer to her. "That may be the most romantic thing anyone's ever said to me."

"Oh, God, give me some time, tiger. I'll sweep you off your feet. But first things first—hang on." She navigates the glass-strewn sidewalk carefully; then she reaches out with her arm and takes my hand. "*Su* ghost *es mi* ghost—got it?"

I place my fingers beneath her chin and gaze deeply into her shadowed eyes. "I'll never forgive myself if you get hurt. What if—"

"What if the sky falls? What if the earth breaks apart beneath our feet? What if everything in existence just winks out, just like that?" Trudy kisses my fingertips carefully, lingeringly, her eyes hot and bright and piercingly alive. "Anything could happen at any time, anywhere. All we can do is follow what makes us happy. And you, Alexandra Dark..." She presses her full length against me, and I slide my hands over the curve of her lower back, teasing at the edge of her panties. "*You* make me happy. So I'm sticking by your side. Whether you like it or not."

"I like it." I kiss her—so hard and so long that we pant against one another for long moments once our mouths part. I try to focus on this, on *us*. All that matters is this moment—here, now, my body and my breath bound to Trudy. Her paper-and-sugar scent, her warmth, all that she is surrounds me, soothes me, and I can only hope that, in some way, my presence reassures her, too.

Forehead tilted against hers, I whisper, "I like it so much that I feel like my heart is breaking."

Her lips curve. "That isn't breaking, silly. That's healing. And sometimes the healing part hurts more than the breaking part. It's happening inside of me, too," Trudy says, placing one of my hands upon the left side of her chest, over her heart. "See? But my not-so-scientific deductions suggest that the pain's going to be worth it in the end. Really, really worth it." She brushes my hair back from my eyes and smiles at me as if I'm her favorite person in the world.

I realize then, in a world-tilting rush, that Trudy is *my* favorite person in the world. And we never would've been drawn together—well, again—if it weren't for my scary old haunted Victorian.

*Everything happens for a reason...*

What if I had laughed off my sister's suggestion to buy this place? I came so close to doing just that. I would still be in Cairo, still spending long, wild nights with Lucia, still leading a disconnected, disinterested existence. It scares me, how much impact one decision can have on the fabric of a person's reality...

I suppose that's how Elizabeth felt when she

realized that Xavier had poisoned her, that he had, in a single, mad moment, spirited her whole future away.

Heart hammering, I remove the black velvet pouch from my pocket. I'm hesitant to open it again, to share its contents with Trudy. It's what we suspected, but to hold this evidence in my hands, to take it in with my eyes, makes everything feel too real, too horrible.

But I can't withhold it from her; Trudy has a right to know.

"I found these in Xavier's dresser," I tell her simply, and then I lay the photographs, face up, on her palm.

There's no mistaking who the figures are. We've encountered Bess and Victoria often enough now to be able to recognize their shapes in any context. And the jagged black oval surrounding the images makes it clear that the photographs were taken through the peephole in Xavier's bedroom. The setting is, unmistakably, the adjoining bedroom, with its fancy bed coverings, the silken robes slung over the bedpost.

As we guessed, Xavier watched Bess and Victoria make love.

Worse, he took *pictures* of them making love. Lovely pictures—if they weren't evidence of his sickness, of his obsession.

Trudy's face contorts into a red-cheeked expression of rage. "What a disgusting, repulsive, slimy—"

"I know. Here, let's put the pictures away." I slide them back into the pouch and return the pouch to my pocket. "Are you all right?"

"Right as rain. I'm actually kind of excited— to bust that ghost's revolting ass. Anyway, c'mon, love—we're holding up a séance." Trudy tugs at her tank top and grins sheepishly. "And *I'm* standing outside in my underwear. I kind of feel like the mom in *Poltergeist* right now. Is she hotter than me?"

"You're hotter. And—thank God—I don't own a TV."

# Chapter Eleven

Constance Reed arrived prepared.

I guess she keeps an emergency séance kit in her hatchback, because she draws item after item out of her Mary Poppins-esque carpet bag, transforming Xavier's shoddy bedroom into a spiritualist den within a matter of minutes. In lieu of a table, she drags the short dresser into the middle of the room and drapes it with a heavy black cloth. And on the cloth, she places a collection of white candles, which she lights one by one. Then she takes a bundle of dried herbs and holds her lighter to the ends of them until they're smoking.

"Sage, to cleanse the space," she explains to Trudy and me as she walks around the room, waving the herbal wand at the ceiling, at the walls.

We watch, silent, flashlights clenched tightly in our hands. The candles cast eerie shadows on our faces, and I can't help but train my light along the floorboards, anxious that one of the mirror shards from the other room might have, somehow, bounced over here.

"Need any help?" Trudy, clad in her Ghost Team jumpsuit once again, offers Constance a small, tight smile.

"No, dear. I'm nearly through." The medium finishes circling the room and places her burning sage in an abalone shell shaped like a bowl. "All right, then.

Could the two of you step up to the dresser, please? We'll have to hold hands."

I turn off my flashlight, putting it on the floor, by my feet. Then I slip my fingers between Trudy's; her hand is cold, colder than mine. But Constance's skin is warm, almost hot, and that reassures me somehow, convinces me that she knows what she's doing. The temperature in the attic is at least ten degrees cooler than the temperature in the rest of the house, so I think Xavier is nearby. He hasn't made his presence known since he exploded the downstairs window. Maybe he's resting, spent for the night—or maybe he's just preparing himself for the big show...

Either way, my heart is beating so hard, I feel as if I've just run a marathon.

Somehow, I keep forgetting to breathe.

Constance closes her eyes and begins to speak in a low, somber voice: "I call upon the four corners—Air, Fire, Water, Earth—for your guidance this dark, still evening. I call upon the white light of the Goddess. Shroud us, Goddess, with your love, with your white light of protection."

My throat is too dry to swallow, and I have to resist the urge to cough. I feel odd, strangled, like I'm choking...

"We call upon the spirits now. Are you here, spirits? Speak to us. Use this vessel"—Constance indicates herself with a nod of her head—"to speak. I welcome you freely. I welcome you to use my tongue to tell us your tale. There is nothing to fear. Within this circle, you are safe, protected—" She cuts her final word short, purses her lips. "Does the name True—no, Truman—does *Truman* mean anything to the two of you?"

"What?" Trudy's jaw drops.

"I'm hearing from someone named Truman. Is he the entity in this house? I don't believe that's the name you used in your voicemail—"

"No, no. Truman..." Trudy pauses, swallows. "Truman is—was my brother. My twin."

"Ah. That explains the resemblance."

"You can *see* him?"

"Of course. He's standing right behind you."

Trudy spins around, letting go of our hands, but there's no one there. She waves her arms, as if she's hoping to grasp hold of him. "What does he look like? What is he saying?" Her voice is thick, as though she's trying to speak around her emotion. I reach out to take her hand again, and she squeezes it gratefully.

"He's blond, and he has magnificent purple eyes. Almost as magnificent as yours, my dear."

Trudy, flushed, ducks her head, lips curving softly. "Well, he had a prettier smile than me. And longer lashes. I was always jealous of his lashes."

Constance takes Trudy's hand, too, and she leans toward her and whispers in a low, soothing tone, "He wants you to know that he's sorry for leaving so soon—"

"Oh, God..." Instantly, Trudy sobs; tears stream from her eyes, gleaming in the firelight.

"—but that he hasn't left you, not really. He says, 'I'm still here, DeeDee.' Maybe you've noticed something, a scent of cucumbers?"

Speechless, Trudy can only nod her head.

"That's him, dear. He's here. And he's not going anywhere without you.'"

"Alex," Trudy whispers, falling into my arms. Her shoulders rock with her sobs as I smooth her hair, kiss her temple. Constance makes eye contact with me above Trudy's head, her lips drawn into a strange, enigmatic smile.

"Your parents are here, too, Alex," she says softly, almost inaudibly.

I stare. It's all I'm capable of doing; everything within me feels as if it's stopped, paused. I'm holding my breath; my heart has ceased beating.

Could it be true? I've waited so long to know that they're all right, that they're in peace. Cordelia told me Jack had had encounters with Dad, and, frankly, I don't doubt that at all, but I never dreamed that I might encounter him, or Mom, myself.

I lick my lips, summon a voice, croak, "They're here?"

"They love you, Alex, so much, and they want you to know that they never felt any pain. There was only light. They don't regret anything; they were happy to go together—though they miss you deeply. And your sister. And Jack. Or—no, they say that they visit Jack. Is Jack in spirit?"

"No. He's...he's their grandson. My sister's son. And"—I laugh hoarsely—"he sees dead people."

"Ah, an angel child."

"What?"

"It's what we call the young mediums. But, my dear, if your nephew is psychic, perhaps the trait is genetic. Maybe you have some natural psychic ability, too. It might explain why you were drawn here, and why the spirits have been so active in your presence."

Cordelia had suggested something similar when she first arrived at V. Rex. But I shake my head, confused, my mouth downturned. I'm overwhelmed by this séance already, and we haven't even delved into the dark, scary stuff. Dread crawls, cold and sharp-nailed, over my skin. What if summoning Xavier's spirit only makes him angrier, stronger? Could a ghost commit murder? He's already proven that he can inflict physical harm...

I don't know what I'm doing.

I don't know what to do.

"Your parents are asking you to move on, to let them go. 'Let us go, Axle.' They have lingered for you; your grief has kept them here. But it's time for them to advance to the next stage of their cycle."

"Cycle?" I blink at Constance, uncomprehending.

"They'll be born again, reincarnated. And if their spirits are bonded, as it appears that they are, they'll find one another again. Maybe they'll even find you."

"Find me? But...they'd be children."

"Yes."

This is too much. I'm not prepared to restructure my personal philosophy *again*, not here, not now. I've come to terms, more or less, with ghosts, but pondering the concept of rebirth will have to wait for another, more suitable time. Still, I have to admit—Constance's communication from my parents has altered something inside of me. When they died, a void took up residence in my chest. I could feel it, could almost *see* it. It was black, jagged, a vacuum, impossible to fill.

But I place my hand over it now, and I know it's different, smaller: a mouse hole rather than a black hole. And if I don't concentrate on it, it almost feels as if it's no longer there at all...

Trudy wipes her face and rests a cool hand on

my cheek before returning to her place behind the dresser. "Sorry for the sobfest."

Constance smiles. "No apologies required. But, yes, we should move on. Let us summon the spirits of the house." She squares her shoulders, and her shadow on the wall behind her, unaccountably, appears to grow taller, wider. "Spirits, we know you are here. We know you are listening. Now is your opportunity to speak, to bridge the gap between the living and the dead. Tell us—"

"Oh!" Trudy gapes at the medium. "Something..." she mumbles, but the word sounds muffled, as if her mouth is stuffed with cotton. She turns her startled gaze toward me, and I lean toward her. "Al—" she begins.

"Trudy, what's—"

"Not Trudy." Every hair on my body stands on end. Because the voice coming from Trudy's mouth is not Trudy's voice, but it is a voice I've heard before.

"She's possessed," I whisper, gasping. My lungs feel as if they're being squeezed by invisible hands. Every breath is a struggle. I begin to wheeze.

"Tell us your name, spirit." Constance is trying to regain control of the situation, but she sounds strained, and her palm, I am anxious to note, is now ice cold.

Trudy's lips part, but they look all wrong. Everything about her looks wrong. She isn't moving like Trudy. She doesn't even *look* like Trudy anymore. She looks like—

"Victoria. My name is Victoria."

"Hello, Victoria." Calmly, Constance nods her head, sloping her body in Trudy's direction. "We're glad that you've joined us tonight. You are welcome here. What is it that you need to say? Go on. You can speak freely now."

Uncomfortable, I shake my head, try to twist my hand free from Constance's, but she holds it fast. "No. No, Trudy never agreed to this. What if—"

"Trudy is safe, well," Victoria informs me with my girlfriend's mouth, even as she focuses her steady blue gaze on me. Blue, true blue, not blue-violet. "She is still here, listening. Don't be afraid, Alex. I would never harm her, nor you. Never." Her eyes soften, and her voice becomes low, husky, thick with emotion: "You remind me of my Bess."

"Your Bess..." The way that she spoke the words—quietly, reverently—made my heart skip a beat. Despite the tight feeling in my throat, I force out, "Why are you and Bess trapped here? Why can't you leave?"

"We were lovers. Sweethearts. Just as you and Trudy are sweethearts." She narrows her brows. "But it was different for us. We had to hide. We couldn't let anyone see us together. We had to be so careful—and, oh, we *were*." As I watch, her jaw clenches, and her gaze grows hard. "But *he* was always watching Bess. And he saw us. He *watched* us. Secretly. Through that hole." Victoria/Trudy turns slightly and points toward the Peeping Tom notch cut into the wall. "We made love in the attic, and he *watched* us. Again and again. Oh, he hated me." Her lower lip trembles. "Because he loved *her*."

I'm about to open my mouth to ask Victoria how we can help her when my last breath is stolen from my lungs. I feel as if I've been punched in the stomach by a wrecking ball. I gaze down at myself, expecting to find that my chest has caved in, that my ribs have collapsed, but, no, I'm okay. I look all right. I just can't *breathe.*

"Alex? Alex!" I hear Constance calling out my name, but she sounds far away, as if she's in another room, or maybe *I'm* in another room, because suddenly everything looks strange, unfamiliar. No, wait—my *eyes* aren't working properly. Or...

A deep, spine-chilling voice fills my head, so loud that it makes my eardrums vibrate: "Thanks for the ride, Alex."

"No," I say, or try to say, but my mouth won't cooperate, doesn't even open—until it *does* open, and, horrified, I listen to it cackle, in Xavier's voice, "I'll do away with you, *whore*—this time, for good!"

"Stop! Wait!" Constance shouts, and I try to turn toward her, try to move at all, but my every gesture is directed by *him*. Oh, God... I've been possessed by Xavier Manderson. The Peeping Tom. The probable murderer.

I've never felt so violated, so filthy from the inside out.

Frantic, I scrabble for control. It's hard to focus on my senses when they're being intruded upon, overridden, and though I can't fully manipulate them, I manage to gain access to my sight again.

And I'm outdoors, standing in the backyard. How did I get here? How long was I struggling for my vision? The night is chilly, quiet, and I stare at my feet, watch in half-despair, half-fascination as they tromp through the mud of their own accord. *Tromp, tromp, tromp*...until they pause beside the pond in the vacant lot. It's only then that I lift my gaze, that I see that my hands—*my* hands—are stretching out, reaching for Trudy's neck. No, Victoria's neck. No, *Trudy's* neck.

If Xavier hurts Victoria, it's Trudy who will

feel the pain.

*No.*

No, this *isn't* going to happen.

I summon every atom within me, every moment of strength I have ever known, or witnessed, every memory of something miraculous—

And my feet stumble backward, away from Trudy/Victoria, who stands glaring in my direction, her arms crossed demurely, her chest heaving with every breath. Constance rushes up behind Trudy and rests her hands on her shoulders. "I banish you, Xavier—"

"Do you?" Xavier, using my throat, my tongue, only laughs. "Well, I'd like to see you try, hag. And, oh, you're a saucy one, Alex. I expected that. But the trollop was only a distraction. A lark. It's all she's good for. No, *you're* the one I'm after. We were fine here, the three of us, until you came and set it all topsy-turvy. Well, time for the valet to take out the trash, hmm? Fancy a swim?"

Cold water soaks my legs. I realize then that Xavier has waded into the pond; the water laps at the top of my thighs, at my waist. How deep does the pond go? Suddenly, my head is plunged underwater—deeper, deeper. I can't fight this. I can't move my arms or my legs. I can't even close my mouth or hold my breath.

I'm going to drown.

*Please...someone...Elizabeth...*

And just like that, I'm *free*.

With a rush of warmth, I realize that Xavier is gone.

Gleeful, I expel the air and water from my lungs, and something—a gentle, coaxing something—urges me to swoop upward, aiming for the air.

When my head surfaces, I gasp, breathing too hard, too fast. But not for long.

"Alex!" The voice is a strange combination of Trudy's and Victoria's, but its panicked tone is unmistakable.

I blink water out of my eyes just in time to see a liquid funnel rotating before me, rising furiously out of the pond. The funnel takes shape, thickens in some places, separates in others, until, at last, it resembles a man. A man made of water, of a hundred-thousand reflections.

"Xavier," I croak, but I hadn't intended to speak at all—and I realize then that I'm not alone in my head.

There's...someone else here.

*It's me, Elizabeth*, the other thinks at me—though I already knew, already felt her close, closer than my own shadow. At some point after Xavier crashed out of me, Elizabeth filtered in. How, I don't know. Why, I couldn't guess. But her habitation isn't invasive so much as familiar, comfortable. And gracious. I still have access to all of my limbs, all of my senses—though, apparently, she can borrow them.

She borrows my hand now—and punches Xavier in the face.

The blow dissipates his water droplets for a moment, but then a strange, gurgling laughter emanates from his form. "You punch like a spoiled rich girl," he snarls. And then a wall of water engulfs me.

I'm drowning. Again. *We're* drowning.

What can I do? How can I—

*Kiss her*, Elizabeth tells me.

Suddenly, like magic, Trudy is in the pond, in my arms. She wraps her legs around my waist and her arms around my neck, and our mouths—despite the water between us—crash together.

And it feels like we're flying.

I'm kissing Trudy, and Trudy's kissing me, but on a different level, Bess is kissing Victoria. Despite time, despite *death*, they're reunited, entwined, and the kiss grows so fevered, so intense, that tears course over my cheeks, and my heart swells like a balloon in my chest.

Oh, my God...

There's so much *love*.

It's dizzying, gravity-defying. It's more powerful than anything I've ever felt before. I'm full, whole, *immortal*.

And when our lips disconnect, all that remains of Xavier is a ring upon the surface of the water, a ring that I break up into little waves with my hand.

"He's gone," Constance whispers from somewhere nearby.

"Yes, he's gone," Victoria agrees, with Trudy's mouth. "As long as we were kept apart, he was able to use us, to drain our energy and hold us captive here."

"And now that we're together..." Bess whispers through me.

"Now that we're together, he's nothing. He's left forever. And we, my love, can leave at last, too."

Constance draws a step nearer, her hazel eyes wide, her beringed hand hovering at her mouth. "This is...astonishing."

"But first... Oh, it's an impolite request, but it's been so long, you see." Bess closes my eyes and fills with me a *whoosh* of gratitude—and then she asks me, by thought alone, to grant her one last wish before she disappears.

"What?" I whisper, jaw gone slack. "But..." Shocked, I open my dripping eyelashes to gaze at Trudy's face, the face that isn't quite hers anymore. Her mouth moves, in a very Trudy-like fashion, into a teasing sideways smile.

"Hey," she says softly, shrugging her shoulders, "who are we to stand in the way of true love?"

"Yeah. I guess..." I lift my brows and laugh hoarsely. "Well, I'm game if you are."

"Totally. This'll make a great chapter in my autobiography."

"No one will ever believe you."

"Not sure I believe it myself, but what the hell? Shall we?" Trudy offers me her wet arm, and after we bid goodbye to a still-gaping Constance Reed—with a promise to return her candles to her through Marie—we traipse out of the pond and across the back lawn together. Then we slosh into the house, walk upstairs, aiming for my—and Elizabeth's— bedroom.

"On second thought..." I raise an eyebrow and reach for Trudy's hand, tugging her toward the open bathroom doorway, instead. And inside of my head, I hear Bess laugh musically, amused, granting her approval.

Then I flick on the chandelier and run the hot water in the clawfoot tub, pouring some rose-scented bath salts beneath the faucet. The steam rises, the sweet perfume fills my nose, and Trudy is in my arms, her skin cool from the night, slick from the pond.

"You made a promise, tiger," she says, her voice velvety. "Remember?" She removes my hand from her back and places it, quite purposefully, on her jumpsuit's zipper. "Wanna help me out of this thing?"

Coursing with adrenaline, I growl my assent, pressing my mouth against her neck as my hand slides beneath the hot pink fabric and finds her peaked nipple. I pinch and pull as my questing lips taste, lick. Then we're kissing—so hard that our teeth clack together, so deeply that I feel all that I am, all that Elizabeth is, mingling with Trudy, with Victoria. It's the oddest sensation, as if I'm kissing two women at once, and yet there's only Trudy before me, only Trudy who grows hot beneath my tongue...

Still holding her, still kissing her, I drag Trudy's zipper down to her bellybutton, teasing her beneath the fabric with my hands, trailing my now-hot fingers along her sides, the curve of her hips, the edge of her panties. Then I ease the jumpsuit off of her shoulders, baring her warm, pink skin; the outfit slips from her arms, falls to her waist, and I fall to my knees, kissing her stomach, pulling the fabric down, down, along with her panties, until she's naked, blushing, panting...

In adoration, I kiss her feet, her ankles, her calves. Her hands caress my hair as my hands caress her knees, as I lick the lean length of her thighs—and then, gently, I coax her legs apart. Trudy cries out as my tongue savors her wetness, her sweetness; there is nothing in this moment but her, only her, and this moment is all times, every time, forever. My nails dig into her backside as her hips begin to move in a rhythm, matching the quick, heated pulsing of my tongue.

"Alex," she sighs, pulling hard at my hair, moaning softly above me, and then not so softly. "Oh, yes..."

I balance on my knees and slide two fingers inside of her; she immediately clenches around me, hot, throbbing, as my tongue teases at her clit—

"Oh!" she breathes, leaning back against the rim of the tub, gripping it with her hands as the waves of pleasure arc through her. I feel them move through her, feel her shock, her pleasure. And when I lift my face to gaze into her eyes, something strange happens: for a moment—and only a moment—it isn't Trudy looking back at me at all. It's Victoria, her long blonde waves loose, her lips swollen and pink, her eyes achingly blue, and when she smiles at me, I wonder who she sees—me, or Bess?

But an instant later, my Trudy is there again, and I rise, stripping off my wet clothes, turning off the faucet. Together, we climb into the water, chest to chest, Trudy lying on top of me, and the sensation of her body floating just above mine, light and grazing, sets me on fire. Our mouths collide, and I feel Trudy's hand moving between my legs, seeking, touching, teasing me. With a mischievous glint in her eye, she dips her head below the water to bite my nipples.

I moan, sinking lower, clutching at her hair, her shoulders.

At last, she lifts her head, laughing. "I suppose this is how mermaids do it. I've always wondered about that. Well, I've wondered more about *this...*" With a sly smile, her arm snakes again along my length until her fingers find me, effortlessly move inside me.

I throw back my head, groaning, and Trudy's mouth claims my throat with a line of hot, possessive kisses. Eyes closed, I can almost imagine that we've fallen though time, that we've traveled back to Bess and Victoria's time, that we *are* Bess and Victoria, seeking any excuse to be alone together, any ploy to steal a private moment, a secret kiss...

Because, though Bess' father adored her, he would never have understood this. Never. Not this. It simply wasn't done, not with this level of seriousness. Girls played with one another, but they didn't fall in love. It was absurd—or so he would claim. And if they were found out, were, inevitably, forsaken by their families, how would they live? How would they survive?

These thoughts aren't mine, but they *feel* like mine, and the emotional impact, the impossibility of Bess and Victoria's love, guts me; hot tears course over my cheeks even as a flood of pleasure crests through my body. I reach for Trudy, search her face; there are tears standing in her eyes, too. I catch them on my fingers, pull her close, as close as two bodies can get... My mouth brushes against her ear.

God, I'm so grateful for her.

I *love* her.

"I love you." The words are a breath, my truest breath, and Trudy covers my mouth with her own, as if to breathe the words in. She relaxes against me, holding me tight as the hot water laps around our shoulders.

"Promise?" she whispers, trailing a wet fingertip from my temple to my mouth.

"Promise." I kiss her finger and sigh.

I've never felt so at ease, so content. So free.

❧❀☙

I wake tangled in Trudy's limbs, deliciously sore, swollen, naked. She opens her eyes sleepily and offers me a lazy grin. "What a night, eh?"

I laugh, nestling against her. "All good horror movies should end like that, I think."

"With hours and *hours* of sex?"

"Basically."

"They aren't here anymore, are they? Bess and Victoria?"

I bite my lip; then I bow my head, thinking. I knew, upon waking, that Elizabeth wasn't inside of me anymore, and I'm guessing that Victoria has left Trudy, too. Their spirits must have drifted off after we fell asleep last night. But the funny thing is...I can still feel them. Close by. In the house. We aren't alone—not yet.

But why?

Then it hits me: "The locket."

"What?"

"We never found the locket. Victoria insisted..." I shake my head, raking a hand through my messy hair as I try to disentangle my thoughts. "I don't think they'll be able to leave until we find it. But I don't know where to look. I've never known. It could be anywhere..."

Trudy, smiling playfully, slips her hand beneath the blankets and touches me, massages me. Her mouth covers mine for a long, toe-curling minute. And then she draws back and lifts a brow. "But *I* do know," she whispers, planting a kiss on my nose. "Victoria was a part of me, inside of my heart, my head. I know her secrets now. And I know..." She pauses, face falling. The light leaves her eyes as she says, "I know how she died."

"Oh." I sit up against the headboard so that Trudy can rest her head on my blanketed lap; my fingers weave in and out of her soft golden curls. "Tell me."

"They were supposed to meet that night, Bess and Victoria, in the Pattons' house. Victoria was excited. She had a gift for Bess. She'd saved her wages for weeks in order to buy it." Trudy smiles, as if she's reminiscing. "She'd considered buying a ring, but rings were for other people, boring people, and Bess was hardly boring. Besides, Bess had told Victoria that she hated rings.

"So Victoria went to McClaren's Jewelry Shoppe and ordered a necklace. A *locket*, engraved on the back. And it had just come in, and just in time, because this was going to be their first weekend alone together. Bess' father and Xavier were overseas, and the cook was visiting her son in Rochester. Victoria had requested time off from work. She'd bought a new hat.

"It was going to be perfect. Like a honeymoon."

I shift uncomfortably, sighing. "But Xavier wasn't overseas."

"No. He wasn't. He'd must have lied to Godrick on the dock, made some excuse. Because he came back into the house, surely startling Elizabeth, and he poisoned her. He killed her. She was already dead by the time Victoria arrived.

"Victoria had a key and let herself in, and Xavier was cruel enough to allow her to seek Bess in the bedroom, to find her lying lifeless there. Victoria screamed, and then Xavier nearly strangled her, but she escaped him, ran...

"She ran all the way to the Bridal Veil Falls."

"Oh, my God."

"I think he herded her there. He wanted the drama. Drama pleased him..."

"He pushed her, didn't he?"

Trudy blinks at me for a long moment, as if she's coming out of a trance. "How did you know?"

"I saw it in a dream. I think Xavier *wanted* me to see it. The monster..." Chilled, I shiver, imagining Victoria—brokenhearted—standing on the edge of the waterfall, confronting the final moments of her life. "So she took the necklace over the falls with her," I say softly.

"No, she didn't."

"What?"

Trudy tilts her head back to gaze at me fondly. "She left it in the house. Dropped it—in an urn Elizabeth had dug out of the ground. In the vain hope that Bess might wake up, might find it."

"You mean—"

"Clever as always, tiger. Yeah. The locket's in Elizabeth's urn at the library. Or...it should be, provided no one's snuck off with it since then."

I fling the covers off of my legs. "Well, let's go!"

Trudy laughs, rolling onto her back. "Are you always so eager in the morning?"

My eyes meet hers, and longing courses through me, as hot as my blood, and my heart seizes unexpectedly in my chest. With slow, deliberate motions, I climb on top of her, my curves fitting snug against her curves, as if one set was custom-made to complement the other. "I meant what I said last night, you know." I lick my lips, kiss her lips. "I love you, Trudy."

"And I love you, you mad, beautiful woman."

My heart beats triple-time in my chest. "You do?"

"Well, let's see. I'd give up all of my books for you. I'd give up all of my *clothes* for you. I'd travel the world for you—"

"You would?"

"In a hot minute, tiger."

I sit up then, wrapping my arms around my knees. "I don't want you to give up anything for me. It isn't fair. And the thing is..." I cast her a sheepish glance over my shoulder. "I think I'm beginning to grow fond of this place."

"This house?"

"Yeah."

"Well..." Trudy sits up behind me, wrapping her arms around my middle, pressing a kiss to my neck. "It'd be awfully nice to have a love nest to come home to—in between adventures, I mean. Hey, you can dig up ancient stuff while I investigate ancient ghosts. I could even write a book... I've always wanted to write a book. Aside from my autobiography, that is."

I reach for her hand and gaze deeply into her eyes. "You're serious? You really want to do this? Travel with me, live with me? Like...for good?"

With expert motions, Trudy swings a leg over my lap and pushes me back down to the pillow, kissing me so long and so hard that we're both left gasping for air. "'Til death do us part." She covers my face, my chest, my body with her kisses.

Again, Marie's words circle through my mind:

*Everything happens for a reason...*

    I wrap my reason in my arms and vow to never take her for granted, to never let her feel, for a single second, anything less than adored.

# Chapter Twelve

Eyes closed, I touch the locket at my throat, relishing the sensation of cool metal upon my hot skin. Behind me, the waterfall crashes against stones, and I feel its mist, hear its roar, its whispers.

How many tragedies have these waterfalls witnessed?

How many love stories?

Trudy slips her damp hand into mine, and I turn toward her, smiling. She's dressed like all of the other tourists at the Cave of the Winds, in a bright yellow poncho to protect her clothes from the ever-present mist. We've walked together down the vertical wooden decks to reach the river and the bottom of the Bridal Veil Falls.

"Just think—this is where I first glimpsed those cunning green eyes of yours." Trudy traces her finger over my mouth and says, "This is where I first tasted your lips. I was only a kid, but I knew what I liked. What I wanted."

"And, as I recall, you *took* what you wanted. Very...assertively."

"Mm. How about a reenactment?" Tugging on my arm, Trudy pulls me beneath the overhanging stones, into the cave-like entrance, and kisses me—hungrily, endlessly—until I'm laughing, dizzy. And then I kiss *her*, holding tight to her arms, breathing her in along with the scent of the water, of the stones, of a hundred-thousand stories...

Her fingers toy with the locket, flipping it over to read the engraving on the back: *B. Yours forever. Cross my heart. V.* They're the same words that Victoria wrote on the note she hid in the conch shell. They must have had a special meaning for the two of them, like a charm, a mantra.

When Trudy and I found the locket in the water flask at the library, we opened it to reveal a lock of Victoria's golden hair. Then, purposefully, as if we were bewitched, we took it back to V. Rex, fetched Elizabeth's hair from Xavier's room, and placed a small curl of it in the locket, too.

And...something happened. It wasn't visible, wasn't even audible. But we both felt it, like a lifting, a lightening. A leaving. Bess and Victoria left, finally, at long last. And Trudy clasped the locket around my neck. I haven't removed it since. Normally, I feel no affinity to jewelry, but the locket's weight against me feels right, meant to be—just as the woman in my arms feels right and meant to be.

I never used to believe in "meant to bes."

I never used to believe in love.

But I thought ghosts were made-up, too. The product of impressionable, hysterical minds. How's that Carl Sagan quote go? *The absence of evidence is not the evidence of absence.* Over the past several weeks, I've had that message pounded into my brain so hard, I don't think any amount of skepticism could dislodge it.

Another thing to be grateful for.

Cordelia's already talking about a backyard wedding, but Trudy and I are more focused on enjoying the moment: right here, right now. Maybe we'll get married someday. Maybe we'll even adopt a dog. Trudy's already picked out a name: Slimer, Slimy for short.

But that's far off, far away. Right here, right now, I'm standing beneath a waterfall with the woman I love, and I want to linger. I want to cherish her—here, now—because, if Bess and Victoria taught me anything, it's that moments are sacred, finite.

And love conquers all.

Love is stronger than hatred, than darkness, than death.

"Alex, look!" Trudy points.

I follow the direction of her arm and blink. There's mist clouding my vision, and we're so far below the viewing ledge. But I could swear... I could *swear* that I see two women wearing Victorian dresses—one black, one white—strolling arm in arm along the railing. They look like the women in my snow globe, heads bent together, whispering to one another, as if they're sharing a secret...

"Alex, is it—"

Just then, the dark-haired woman turns her head and peers over the railing, staring pointedly in our direction. She's smiling. No, *beaming*.

"They're saying goodbye," I whisper, as I smooth my thumb over the locket at my throat.

"Goodbye," Trudy breathes, wrapping her arm around my waist.

The women move onward, but their feet no longer seem to quite touch the ground, and as they rise higher and higher, I notice, amused, that Elizabeth is wearing her showy red boots.

Hmm. I wonder if *I* could pull off a pair of red boots... I glance down at my feet, at the old, worn boots that have accompanied me to hundreds of dig sites—and to dozens of cots. These boots represent someone I no longer identify with, no longer know. And Cordelia once told me that red is my color...

The ghosts dissipate into the mist, or maybe they become the mist, my mother's water dust. The space they occupied against the sky flickers, for just an instant, with a rainbow.

"Oh..." Trudy regards me with shining violet eyes, her face stained with tears. "They're together. Alex, they're *together*. They're safe. It's beautiful."

"You're beautiful." I press a kiss to her salty-sweet mouth, weaving my arm through the crook of her elbow. We move off of the rocks and ascend the staircase, and with each step, I feel as if I'm sealing a promise. A promise to Trudy—and to myself.

A promise to be brave and vulnerable. To love wildly but softly. To trade my skepticism for possibility, my stubbornness for compromise, my solitude for companionship, my aloofness for love.

With Trudy's warmth by my side, her cotton candy scent tickling my nose, I know that it's a promise I'll never falter on, never, ever break. Not for all the treasure in Egypt.

Cross my heart.

## *The End*